WRITTEN BY: KEVIN WHITAKER

www.mcclurepublishing.com

Cover Design Images by: KREW ENTERTAINMENT LLC.

Interior Layout by Kathy McClure

http://www.mcclurepublishing.com

To order additional copies, please contact
books@mcclurepublishing.com
800-659-4908

In Loving Memory of my sister
Nicola 'Nikki' Matthews

Acknowledgements

Krew Entertainment Group, McClure Publishing, Inc., L. Johns Law Group, Live Club Link, Western Auto Repair, Men@Large, LeClaire Community, B. Moore Consulting Inc. Kell's Dougie, Parker Trucking, The Tate Brothers, M.O.B., Corner Crew, Will Do Krew, 45th Lawler Click, Marlene's Beauty Salon, and Buns Unlimited Inc.

SPECIAL THANKS:

To God for blessing me with a loving family and friends, Dr. A. Johnson and family, my sisters Karla, Yvette, Ashley, and brothers Victor and Gerald. My daughters Tara, Felicia, Kiandra, Natasha, Kyleishia, Cindy, my name sake Kevin Whitaker Jr., My Auntie Edna Fuller and family, The Whitakers family, Uncle Ted, Uncle Ralph, Uncle James, Auntie Velma, Auntie Wakanda, Auntie Evonne, The Whitaker in (St. Louis, Kansas City and Chicago,) Bernina McKennie (Editor), Leyte Holliday (artist) and family, Simona (Bambina) Jackson (model) and family, Dave Tolliver (R&B singer) and Edgar (Gemini) Porter, Mrs. M. Boulware and family, Ramona Hopkins and family, Mrs. V. West and family, Mrs. Esther Singleton and family, Mr. and Mrs. Noble, Herb Coleman, Roslyn Carson and family, Eddo, ES Blue, Dreek, Quik-Mix-Claude, DJ Jermaine (The Gentleman), DJ. Eight-Ball, DJ Art, Jay Honey, and a host of others. To all my people who have supported my craft MUCH LOVE TO YOU AND MAY GOD CONTINUE TO BLESS YOU.

"**Scorn**" is a love story that touches home for many. Sheila Fox is the mother of three boys, who will do everything in her power to keep her marriage with Eddie Sr. who is a real estate broker that owns and operates his own company. Eddie Sr. loves his family, but the excitement of the streets keeps him out late away from his family. Eddie Sr. has taken things one step too far, and Sheila cannot put up with it anymore. She wants him to come home and be the man of the house. However, Eddie Sr. does not have the strength to overcome the nightlife and all the temptations of the streets.

This story is fiction but comes across in the most realistic form.

"*Scorn*" is the nightlife versus home life; Lust, alcohol, and friends versus love, peace, and happiness with family. This drama filled story will keep you anticipating what's to come in the complications of relationships captivating your heart.

INTRODUCTION

One cold spring evening Eddie Sr. returns home from one of his overnighters. The door opens quickly with a strong wind as if a force of power pushed it. In comes Eddie Sr. escorted aggressively by three brawly men wearing black hooded jackets. One of the men rushes into the kitchen grabbing Sheila. The gunman takes her into the living room with Eddie Sr. and their three sons. The gunmen all have their pistols drawn pointing the three caliber pistols toward Sheila and the children. Blue, the largest of the three gunmen, approaches Eddie who is standing at 6'2 and 350 pounds is caught off guard.

"I'm going to give you a chance to save a life by giving me the money."

Eddie shaken up pauses, "What money?"

Red, the second in command, pulls out duct tape and begins taping Eddie's family.

"Now, I'll ask you again, where is the money? Nobody has to get hurt," Blue said calmly. Eddie Sr. drops his head in disbelief, "What money?"

Blue smiles, "Have it your way," Blue says furiously, "Red tape all their fucking mouths and bring the Bitch over here."

Red tapes Eddie's three boys' mouths and grabs Sheila shoving her down on the couch in front of Blue.

Tears run down Eddie's youngest son's face, Victor, as he watches his mom get tossed around. Blue growing impatient cracks his neck, "Tell me where the money is or watch me bring pain to your wife."

Eddie Sr. remains silent.

Blue leans over snatching Sheila up off the couch by her shirt and bra. Sheila's shirt rips and her bra pops loose exposing her right breast. She falls down covering herself. E.J., the oldest of the boys, starts breathing heavily as tears stream down his face. Eddie Sr. looks at the fear in his family's eyes.

Blue laughs and leans over and begins rubbing the gun around and between Sheila's breasts. He grabs her hair sticking the gun to her head.

The third gunman, Whitey, standing close to E.J. slaps him in the head with his pistol. E.J. screams out from under the duct tape.

"Time out for playing games, this shit just got real," Whitey exclaimed.

Eddie quickly stands towering over the much smaller guy Whitey to defend his son.

Red cuts Eddie off in his tracks aiming the gun at his head, "Now sit your wanna be tough ass down or watch your family die or they can watch you die."

Eddie Sr. falls back into his seat with fierce eyes.

"Now that you know we mean business, where is the money for the last time?" Blue asked hastily.

Eddie Sr. ponders for a moment not saying a word before he blurts out. "It's not here. Please don't hurt my family. Please!" Eddie Sr. answered.

"Okay, then where is it?" Blue asked.

Eddie Sr. filled with emotions, "It's … it's up north."

Sheila lies on the couch with her shirt open with a blank look on her face. Eddie pleads with Blue, "Man! I can pay you more than the guy who sent you here."

Blue smirks, "Oh, and you will before I am done with you."

Blue lowers his weapon and pulls out his cell phone. He calls the getaway driver Pinky.

"Hey Pinky, pull around. The money ain't here."

Blue hangs up the phone, pulls Eddie up off the couch.

"Yo. Eddie, me and you are about to take a little ride up north."

Blue pushes Eddie Sr. towards the door.

"Here's your chance to save your family. Red, you and Whitey chill until I get back. If this chump knows what's best, he'll just give me the dough."

ONE YEAR BEFORE

The Fox family is a middle class family living in Chicago. Eddie Sr. is 33 years of age and a Real Estate Broker. His wife, Sheila, is 31 years old and a full-time student at Chicago State University. Sheila and Eddie are the parents of three boys, Eddie Jr. (E.J.), 13, Roosevelt, seven, and Victor, five. Sheila is at home preparing dinner for her family when she notices how late it's getting. Sheila is thinking to herself, *Eddie's late again.* Sheila yells down in the basement for the boys, "Boys, it's time for dinner. Cut that game off, and wash your hands before you come to this table!"

The boys hesitant to turn-off the game, stands with the remote in their hands placing the game controller on pause believing that they can continue playing after dinner. One after the other rushes into the bathroom to clean up for dinner. Sheila says, "Okay boys, Eddie Jr. will say grace since your dad is not home again."

After dinner, Sheila helps the boys with their homework as she stacks the dishes in the dishwasher. She allows the boys to play for one hour after finishing up their homework. Sheila cleans up the kitchen while listening to her iPod. Once the kitchen is down, she directs the boys to take a bath and get ready for bed. Sheila looks at the clock. It is just a little after 9:00 p.m. and no Eddie. She sits on the bed, picks up the cordless phone, and begins dialing Eddie's cell phone. When she gets to the last digit, she hangs the phone up. Sheila walks over to the mirror, pulls her hair back into a ponytail, and then walks to the connecting bathroom to run some water for a bath. She adjust the temperature of the water adds some bath beads. She dims the light trying to set the mood. When Sheila returns to the bedroom, she could hear the boys playing around in their room. She heads right down to the boys' room quickly! Trying to surprise them, she busts right in. The boys all appear to be asleep, but the youngest boy, Victor. He has a big smile on his face. Sheila runs over to Victor, kissing and blowing in his face. Victor starts cracking up laughing, "Okay, Mom, okay! I'm going to sleep!"

Sheila stops kissing on Victor and walks over to kiss E.J. and Roosevelt. "Now you boys go to sleep or no video games tomorrow."

"Okay, Mom," E.J. replied.

The boys all lie down, and Sheila closes the room door. She realizes that the water in the tub is still running. She moves quickly to the bathroom, catching the water just before it was about to run over. Once the water is turned off, Sheila walks back into the bedroom stands in front of a full-size mirror and starts to undress. She stands in the mirror admiring her butt and breasts while taking a hard look at her stomach. She grabs her breasts slightly lifting them up as if she was on an episode of Nip Tuck. Sheila grabs her waistline pulling her stomach tight and frowns. Speaking out loud to herself, "Girl, you have got to do something about that little pouch," looking at her naked body.

Sheila turns and walks back into the bathroom glancing at the clock. It's 9:40 p.m. and Eddie has not shown up. Continuing on into the bathroom she opens the medicine cabinet, grabs her razor and shaving gel. After applying the shaving gel to her underarms and vagina, she turns on the water in the sink and starts to remove the hair from her underarms rinsing after each stroke until all the hair has been removed. She leans over and flips the toilet seat up and spreads her legs, one on each side of the toilet, squats down and begins to remove the hair from her vagina. Being very cautious, she swipes and rinses until all the hair has been removed. Once all the hair has been removed, she cups her hand across her vagina checking for spots, her vagina is smooth. She stands and wipes down the seat of the toilet and flushes it. Sticking one foot into the tub checking the water temperature, Sheila slides down in her hot bubble bath. While soaking, Eddie Sr. walks in the bathroom to take a piss. Eddie never said one word to his wife. Sheila stares at Eddie trying to get his attention by splashing water in the tub. Eddie flushes the toilet, washes his hands, and walks out of the bathroom. Moments later, Sheila enters the bedroom wearing a towel around her. Eddie has already taken his clothes off and warmed his dinner. Sheila stands in front of the mirror wrapping her hair. She lets her towel drop exposing her naked body. She tries to tease Eddie by bending over putting on her thong and bra. Eddie lies back on the bed as if Sheila was not even in the room with him. Sheila lotions up and puts on just a hint of perfume with a sheer robe. She climbs in the bed with Eddie kissing him on the cheek. Eddie gives her a hard, angry stare. She backs up thinking to herself "not again," turns and pulls the covers over her.

The next morning, Sheila awakes to find that Eddie has already left the house. One hour later, Sheila is seen rushing the boys off to school. At the school, Sheila hugs and kisses all the boys then speeds off in her SUV going to school herself. In Chicago State student's parking lot, Sheila runs into her girlfriend, Jennifer. Jennifer is slightly younger than Sheila. Sheila pauses for a second.

Jennifer stops beside her.

"Hey, Girl! I see I'm not the only one late today," Sheila stated.

Jennifer with a big smile on her face, "I guess you're not. What are you looking for?"

Sheila flips all around her purse, "Here it is my cell-phone." They pick up the pace.

Sheila checking out Jennifer's gear, "Girl, you know that outfit is poppin'."

Jennifer checks out herself with the once look over. "Not bad, I guess. My man picked this outfit."

Sheila gives a look of confusion. "What man? I thought you told me you were single."

Jennifer grins, "Oh! I thought you knew."

As they start towards the building, Sheila replies, "Knew what?"

Jennifer answers, "Any man buying and not getting any of this cookie is my man."

Sheila cracks up laughing. "Okay, Girl. Sooner or later he is going to want some of that sour dough cookie."

They both start laughing as they enter the building.

Later on that evening, Sheila is sitting on the bed watching the clock it's 9:45 p.m. Eddie comes walking in with a gym bag. He kicks his shoes off. Sheila gets up, walks into the bathroom to get his bath water ready. While Sheila is checking the water, Eddie creeps up and grabs her from behind.

Sheila startled, "Oh Shit!"

Eddie starts laughing.

Sheila shaken up, "Don't be doing that."

Eddie kisses her on the cheek, "I'm sorry." He leans over into the tub removing the stopper, flips on the shower. He begins kissing Sheila on the back of her neck. Eddie starts removing Sheila's clothes.

Sheila replies, "I've already showered."

Eddie fully naked, "Not with me." He continues to undress her.

They both enter the shower. Sheila's washing Eddie's back, and he's rubbing all over her. She kisses his back, and he turns around. She kisses his chest. Eddie grabs the towel and washes her up. She spreads her legs as he wipes gently. He turns her ass to his manhood as she rinses off. He bends her over in the shower entering her hot wetness as he pulls her hair and smacks that wet ass.

Sheila opens her eyes feeling fabulous after a great night with Eddie, finds that Eddie is not lying next to her.

It's a hot day and very bright out on this Saturday morning. Eddie's up in the room talking with the boys. E.J. asks, "Dad, are you going to make it to my baseball game today?"

Eddie looks E.J. in the eyes, "I promise I'll be there."

Roosevelt blurts out, "They never win."

E.J. pushes his brother, Roosevelt. Eddie breaks them apart, "Alright, I told you about fighting each other. Now get ready, I'm taking the family out for breakfast."

Victor smiles at his dad, "Dad, are we going to Mickey Dee's?"

"Boy, your Uncle Reggie got you sounding just like him. It's McDonald's," Eddie replies. They walk into a very nice breakfast restaurant. The boys are well behaved and other families just could not help but notice how well behave the boys are. An older couple approaches Eddie's table.

"I couldn't help but notice how well dressed and behaved these little gentlemen are," the woman said.

Sheila smiles, "Yes, these are momma's little men."

Eddie unfazed by the conversation just kept eating. "I didn't want to interrupt you. It's just rare that you see a family all together. What a beautiful sight." The older woman said. Her husband never said a word he just nodded in agreement when his wife spoke.

After breakfast the family returns home. Eddie goes into his pocket pulling out a large amount of cash, as Sheila sits on the bed. Eddie lays the money on the night stand. Sheila leans forward, grabs the money to count it, "So what is this for?" with a very bad attitude.

Eddie gathering his things to leave out, "It's for whatever you choose to spend it on."

Sheila being nosey, "Where are you off too?"

Eddie chuckles, "It's time to make the doughnuts."

Sheila gives a fake laugh, "Ha Ha! Me and the boys are going to mom's for my nephew's birthday party. I guess you forgot, huh?"

Eddie grabs his car keys, "Nope! That's why I gave you the money to buy him a gift. Pick something up for the boys while you're out shopping."

"Yeah, whatever! Are you coming to E.J.'s game today?" Sheila asked.

Eddie paused before walking out of the bedroom, "I told him I'd be there. Then I'll be there."

Later that afternoon at Sheila's parents' house, Sheila and the boys walk into the backyard. The barbecue grill is going, and the music is pumping so loud Sheila heard it when she pulled up. The yard is decorated with all kinds of birthday banners on this extremely hot day. Sheila has on a nice sundress with some Prada® sandals. As Sheila looks around the yard, most of the women are wearing low-rise jeans with sleeveless tops. Sheila frowns when she sees one of her niece's thong showing. The boys are running all around like mad men. Victor comes up to Sheila crying. She reaches down to pick up her youngest son. "What's wrong, Baby?"

Victor trying to talk through his tears, "I...I...I fell."

One of her brother's friends, Bryant, walks over behind her. Sheila smells his cologne and turns in his direction. Bryant speaks, "Hey, Sheila."

Sheila speaks, "Hello!" as she tries to pamper Victor. "Boy hush!"

Bryant, 25, handsome, wearing urban Hip Hop gear leans forward towards Sheila, "So where is your husband?"

Sheila offended, "Excuse me!" She turns and walks away with her son, Victor, in her arms. Shanae walks over dancing to the music, grabbing Victor's hand while Sheila is holding him.

Shanae dancing, "Come on, Vic, dance with your cousin." Shanae, 22, with three children, but you could not tell by the way she looked. Her body is still tight. She dances doing the latest moves the Q'uan then she starts doing the Whip playing around holding Victor's arms out. Bryant makes his way back over to where Sheila is standing.

Bryant smiles, "So where did we leave off?"

Sheila replies, "We didn't."

Bryant extends his hand, "Well, let me introduce myself properly. I'm Bryant."

Sheila gives him a long, hard stare, and extends her hand, "I'm Sheil…."

Bryant cuts her words off, "Sheila, I know who you are."

Sheila surprised. "Oh! You do?" She cheeses, "And why are you over here again bugging me when all these young single women are back here? And besides, you're a little young with your Sean John gear on. Really! Guys are wearing Robin's Jeans® or at least True Religion®."

Bryant hesitates, "Naw I got the designer Robin Jeans, but none of these girls are my type. I like sophisticated women like you."

Sheila grins, "Not only are you cute, but you know how to compliment a woman. I must admit, it's rare in your generation, but I'm happily married."

Bryant sarcastically says, "Oh yeah! Where is he then?"

Sheila defensively states, "None of your damn business!" Sheila walks away with a bitter look on her face.

Shanae approaches her, "Auntie Sheila, what's up?"

Sheila answers, "Not a damn thing!"

"Why is that fool, Bryant, looking over here like he lost something?" Shanae asked. Shanae stares Bryant down. "He must don't know; Uncle Eddie will have his block knocked off."

"Girl, don't even worry about that boy. He still has milk behind his ears," Sheila replies.

Shanae starts laughing. "Auntie Sheila, I never really understood what that saying meant."

Sheila laughs, "Then why are you laughing?"

"I always knew it was meant to be funny," replies Shanae.

Sheila begins cracking up. "Girl, you're crazy!"

"I've seen him before not sure where." Sheila said.

"He is Bernard's little brother from the corner house two blocks over."

"REALLY! Bernard was one fine brother before he started smoking that crack. He had a good job and all the girls. Now I see why Bryant looks familiar. He has those same light brown eyes."

Shanae quickly responds, "NO Aunt Sheila. Don't get it twisted he got light brown eyes because he's full of shit, and he is a blunt head."

"Wow, is he that bad?" Sheila asked.

"Probably worse," Shanae stated.

"Anyway let me get these boys over to E.J's baseball game. Let me go over and talk with Momma and Dad before they start tweaking."

"E.J. really looks nice in his baseball uniform Auntie, but can he play?"

"He is pretty darn good. You and the boys should come out to watch one of E.J.'s games. Who knows maybe one of your boys can join the team when they get a little older."

"Not today. My boys are going to play basketball."

Sheila gives Shanae a dumbfounded look, "Huh?"

"Yeah basketball," Shanae repeated.

"Okay whatever. You had better let those boys choose what sport they want to play if any."

Shanae fantasizes for a moment, "Yep! One of them can be just like Derrick Martell Rose the MVP of the NBA in 2011."

"Girl you play too much! You're 5'4 and your baby daddy is 5'5 get real!"

"Auntie Sheila gone to E.J's game. I see you been drinking that Hater Aid." Shanae starts laughing.

Sheila yells out, "E.J.!!! Let's go boy before you are late. Nana you're 22 with three boys I really don't know who Derrick Martell Rose is because I don't follow sports like that. However, I do know Prada® and Gucci mixed with some Martell."

Shanae burst out with laughter, "Auntie you're crazy and your outfit is on fleek."

"Okay maybe, but I'm gone. Bye ... everybody! Oh shit! Where is Quincy? I almost forgot to give him his gift."

Quincy turns seven wearing his little birthday hat, runs towards Auntie Sheila with his arms open wide. Sheila bends down to scoop up her great nephew. She kisses his face and he grins with a big grin and laughter.

"Guess what I got for you?" Sheila asked.

Quincy shrugs his shoulders with a big smile.

"More love!" She starts to tickle and kiss him.

Quincy with tears of joy and laughter is enjoying his Great Auntie Sheila. He grabs her around the neck trying to catch his breathe.

"Okay baby get down."

Sheila places Quincy down digging into her Prada® bag pulling out a birthday card. "Here you go Sweetie."

Shanae smiles at her oldest son Quincy. "Go put it by the birthday cake."

"Thanks Auntie Sheila." Quincy walks over to the table where the cake is sitting.

"Girl, love you all. See you later. Tell mom and dad I'll call them later."

Sheila grabs the boys and leaves the party.

Later that evening back at home with the boys Sheila is sitting in the living room while the boys watch television. Eddie strolls right passed them on his way to the bedroom with Sheila on his heels. Eddie tosses his gym bag on the floor. Sheila stares at him in disbelief. "Eddie! Why would you tell E.J. that you were coming to his game and not show up?"

Eddie continues taking off his clothes. "Look, I've had a long day already. I don't need this right now."

Sheila sits on the bed. "Okay. So how was your day?"

Eddie answers, "Very tiring."

Sheila starts to unpack Eddie's gym bag. "Man, these clothes are wet. You must have had a good workout?"

"It was tiring just like I said," replies Eddie.

Sheila asks, "Do you want me to run you some bath water?"

Eddie grabs the remote and sits on the bed in his boxer briefs. "No, I've showered already."

"The party was really nice. Quincy really enjoyed his birthday," Sheila said.

Eddie asks, "Did he like his gift?"

"Yes, he did, but it would have been much nicer if you gave it to him," Sheila replies.

Eddie grins. "For who? Him or you? Oh well, you can't have the best of both worlds. Besides, I'll see the family on the fourth."

Sheila sucks her teeth, "Oh, is that so? You always say you're coming to family gatherings and find some way not to make it." Sheila playfully tries to pull away. Eddie pulls the hair off of her neck and begins kissing and licking on her. Eddie slides her sundress off of her shoulders. Sheila's breasts are exposed, and Eddie takes one of them into his mouth as he slides her underwear off. Sheila fights with Eddie playfully. "The kids are awake," Sheila said knowing all the time she wanted to make love. Eddie continues to run his hands all over Sheila's body until she couldn't resist. He pins Sheila to the bed with one hand and removes his boxers brief with the other hand. He lies on top of Sheila kissing her ever so passionately.

* * *

One month later, at the Harris family barbecue, Eddie pulls up in front of the Harris home with Sheila and the boys. Eddie's styling hard in his new Range Rover truck. The block is watching as Eddie and the family exits his truck. The family has not seen much of Eddie since he lost 60 pounds. The boys exit running to their grandmother Jean. Grandma Jean greets them with hugs and kisses. Eddie helps Sheila get the food she prepared out of the back of the truck. The boys are looking sharp wearing the latest hip hop fashion and Eddie Sr. gear is tight, and Sheila is looking flawless wearing a Prada® skirt and top. They all walk to the back where the family is playing cards, drinking, cooking, and the music blasting. Sheila scans the backyard looking how big everyone has grown. Some of her relatives she has not seen in years came out this year. Sheila's niece, Tonya, approaches her. Tonya reaches out excited to see her aunt, "Hey, Auntie Sheila!"

Sheila smiles as she reaches out to embrace her niece. "Hey Sweetie!" Sheila kisses Tonya on the cheek, "So how are you doing?"

"I'm fine," replies Tonya.

Sheila steps back, "You have grown up to be a beautiful young woman."

Tonya cheesing, "Thank you."

As they speak, Bryant makes his way over bouncing to the music with a beer in his hand. Bryant pumping his fist in the air, "Damn! That's my shit right there," continues pumping his fist to the music as he passes by Sheila and Tonya, "Woo … Hey, Sexy!" looking at Sheila. She looks right pass him as if he was not speaking to her.

Tonya laughs, "I know you see my Uncle Eddie up in here? You had better be talking to me."

Bryant continues, looking at Sheila. Eddie walks up behind Sheila. Tonya rolls her eyes at Bryant when Eddie steps up. Eddie speaks, "Hello Tonya!"

Tonya speaks with excitement in her voice just to irritate Bryant look and says, "Hi, Uncle Ed!"

Eddie questions Tonya, "How is school coming along? I heard you wanted to be a lawyer?"

Tonya smiles, "Yes, it's true. I'm going to be a lawyer."

Eddie responds, "That's good for you. Sheila let me talk with you for minute," as he grabs the back of Sheila's arm.

Sheila steps away with Eddie Sr. "Ouch Eddie! You're hurting my arm! Let me go dammit!"

Eddie Sr. pulls Sheila to the side, "If you were going to invite your little boyfriend, why did you ask me to come?"

Sheila angry, pulls her arm away, "I didn't bring or invite anybody but my family! If you want to leave, just leave! Don't make excuses! Just go!"

Everyone is looking in their direction. Eddie turns loose Sheila's arm. The youngest of the boys, Victor, runs over holding on to Sheila's leg. "Call me when you're ready to go home," Eddie Sr. storms off.

Sheila upset, "Whatever! Now gone to that other bitch you've been spending all your time with!" Eddie Sr. just keeps walking as Sheila yells. "I'm getting tired of this shit."

Victor starts crying. Sheila reaches down to pick him up. "Ssshhh, boy," as she rocks him. "Hush your mouth little boy."

Eddie Sr. walking toward the truck when Sheila's oldest brother Reggie stops him. "What it do, brother-in-law? Let a playa hold something!"

Eddie Sr. gives him a short look and keeps walking.

Reggie bitter, "Punk Mother Fucker!"

Bryant sitting on the steps grits his teeth, "Man, who that chump think he is? Trying to ruin the family cookout," sipping his beer.

Reggie replies, "Hold up, home boy, that's still my brother-in-law. He takes damn good care of my people."

Bryant mean mugs Reggie. "So, Reggie, you think he's cool huh?" He finishes off the contents of his bottle with one big gulp, "Ahhh!"

Reggie replies, "No doubt! Big Ed looks out for the family, not just my sister."

Bryant and Reggie walk back to the yard with the rest of the family. Sheila is holding Victor, rocking him back and forth trying to calm him. Her niece, Shanae, walks up. "Hey! Auntie Sheila, you want me to take Vic while you change clothes?"

Sheila upset. "Change clothes for what?"

Shanae looks down at her skirt and reaches for Victor.

Sheila takes a look down at her skirt. "Dammit! I've got mud all over my skirt."

Shanae puts Vic down. "Vic, I don't want you to get mud all over me, okay?" She puts Victor down holds his arms up dancing to the beat. "Hey now, look at my little cousin. Victor dances with Shanae as other family members form a circle around Victor. The D.J. plays the Bus Stop by Charlie Greene. All the women in the yard get up and join in with Shanae doing the bus stop. The family who were playing cards even bop their heads to the beat and looked on. E.J. being the oldest grandchild is in the front as the older family members chant for E.J.,

"Go E.J. get it baby."

Grandma Jean just smiles looking at E.J.

Reggie and Bryant grab a couple brews out of the cooler and crack open the bottles. Reggie checks the meat on the grill as he bops his head to the beat.

Sheila very upset starts for the house with tears in her eyes.

Sheila is inside the house going through one of her bags. She pulls out a Baby Phat® outfit and heads for the bathroom. She kicks her shoes off as she stands in the mirror. She slides her jeans on under her skirt then removes her skirt. She turns towards the bathroom door standing in her bra and jeans to catch Bryant watching her. Sheila stares at him as she puts her Baby Phat® t-shirt on quickly. Sheila's brother, Reggie, walks in. "Man! What the fuck? Bee, I told you to stay the fuck away from my sister." He grabs

Bryant's throwback Bears' jersey and pulls him away from the bathroom.

Bryant replies, "Slow down, Dawg. I'm leaving. I came in here to take a leak. Stop pushing me, Dawg!"

Reggie slightly irritated, "Or what?"

Bryant, "I'm just saying, Dawg, don't!"

Reggie, "Get the fuck out of my mother's house. Fool, never threaten me in my house. I'll put that work in Fool! Try me."

Bryant, "Yeah yeah! Whatever Reg, when the last time you put some work in? I'm that nigga. It don't even have to go like this."

Reggie angry, "Yeah, but it did! Now what?"

Bryant walks out the door into the backyard. Reggie talks with Sheila.

Reggie concerned. "Sis, you alright?"

Sheila putting her shoes on, "Yes, I'm okay, but I'm glad you came in here. I'm not sure what was on his mind. He must have followed me inside the house.

Reggie, "Me either, but it won't happen again. On the real Bryant has been acting real thirsty lately."

Sheila pulls her hair back into a ponytail. "Don't worry about it. Let's just go back and enjoy the cookout."

They return to the party. Everyone is having a good time taking pictures with their cell phones. The card game is live. The kids are having a water balloon fight. It's getting late, and the bugs are coming out. People are swatting at bugs and starting to leave. Shanae talks with her Auntie Sheila. "Auntie, if you ever want a break from the boys just call me. I don't mind giving you and Uncle Eddie a break."

Sheila slightly laughs, "Tis! Why would he need a break? But I do appreciate the offer, and I'll definitely keep that in mind. So where is that sister of yours?"

Shanae, "Well, you know how Ms. Thang be rocking. She's probably at one of her bougie girlfriends' house studying. She left right after Eddie."

Sheila's phone rings. She looks at the caller ID. It's Eddie Sr. She looks at Shanae. "Speak of the devil. It's Eddie." She answers, "Hello!"

Eddie Sr. politely says, "Hey, Babe! You ready to go home?"

Sheila, "Yes, I am. Where are you?"

Eddie Sr. replies, "I'm in front of your parent's house. The boys are in the truck already."

Sheila, "That's good. I thought I was going to have to look for them. They should be good and tired. I'll be right out. Let me say my goodbyes, and I'll be right out."

Eddie, "Okay Sweetie, can you grab me a plate?"

Sheila, "I guess so, Honey. Bye." Hangs up the phone gives Shanae a real strange look. "I swear to you Shay that Eddie Sr. is bipolar."

Shanae laughs, "I thought you were mad at Eddie, but evidently not with all that (mimics Sheila,) 'Oh, I guess so, Honey!' What was all that?"

Sheila smiles, "Maybe one day you'll understand when you're married. It's about picking and choosing your battles."

Shanae, "Hhhhmmm! Is that what you think? I wear the pants in my relationships."

Sheila replies, "And that's why they don't fit. It's a give and take relationship at times."

They walk towards the house. Shanae, "I know. I give the orders and he takes them."

Sheila laughs, "Girl, you're crazy!" Sheila goes in, gathers her things, and prepares a plate for Eddie. She kisses and hugs everybody. Sheila makes her way down the stairs to the truck with her brother, Reggie. Reggie hugs Sheila before she steps into the truck. Eddie Sr. speeds off and taps the horn. Inside the truck, Eddie Sr. reaches over and grabs Sheila's hand. Sheila smiles reaches to turn the volume down on the radio, "Eddie, what's different about our relationship?"

Eddie Sr. looks in the rearview mirror to see the boys are all asleep. Eddie Sr. answers, "Nothing. Why? What do you think is different?"

Sheila smirks, "Nothing. Maybe I am over exaggerating."

Eddie Sr. glances at Sheila, "Yeah! Maybe huh?"

Sheila answers, "We just don't spend time together like we used to, and I miss those walks in the park." Eddie Sr. does not say a word. Sheila closes her eyes and falls asleep. Eddie Sr. turns the volume back up slightly as he grooves to a classic by Men at Large. A half hour later, Eddie Sr. wakes Sheila with a kiss. Sheila wakes up and asks, "Are we home already?"

Eddie Sr. answers, "No." Sheila looks around to see him outside of the truck with the door open. Eddie Sr. grabs her hand leading her out of the truck. Sheila steps out of the truck, "What are we doing at Grant Park?"

Eddie Sr. replies, "You said that you missed those walks in the park so here we are." Eddie Sr. pulls Sheila close as they both lean back on the truck admiring the sight. He embraces her from behind as they look out on Lake Michigan under the moon light. Sheila and Eddie Sr. are both enjoying the moment. Eddie Sr. slides his hands under Sheila's breasts cuffing them with both hands. She crosses her arms over Eddie's hands holding his hands in that position.

"Do you remember all the things we done before we had our second child?" Sheila asked.

Eddie Sr. reminisces on how they use to go out to dinner with friends. They would have a good time then come home and make love all night. "Yes, I do." He begins kissing Sheila's neck very gently before licking and kissing on her ear. At that very moment blue lights could be seen flashing and a voice rang out, "The Park is now closed. People get in your cars or you'll be ticketed and towed."

Sheila spends around in Eddie's arms giving him a very passionate kiss while holding the back of Eddie's head down. "I love you Eddie."

"I love you too Sheila." They kiss again briefly. Eddie Sr. opens the door as Sheila steps inside, he slaps her ass. Sheila smiles, "What was that for?"

"Because I love the way it sounds and feels." Eddie Sr. replied. Sheila gazes over the seat looking at the boys sleep as Eddie Sr. drives off. She reaches over and grabs Eddie's hand.

Eddie Sr. has been coming home every night for two weeks straight. Sheila has been cooking dinner every night for the family. Sheila and the boys love the time Eddie Sr. is spending with them.

That Saturday morning, Eddie Sr. rolls over getting out of the bed quickly. Sheila reaches over to grab him after a long night of passion Sheila wants more. Eddie Sr. continues to get out of bed. Sheila rolls over to look at the clock. It's 6:30. She pulls off the covers revealing part of her naked body, speaking softly, "Eddie, where are you going this early?"

Eddie Sr. stands there naked as Sheila watches his manhood hanging in front of her. Sheila notices Eddie Sr. frowns slightly when she removes the cover exposing her midsection. Her feelings are hurt but she does not let on. Eddie Sr. grabs a t-shirt and underwear and replies, "I have something to take care of at the office this morning."

Sheila asks, "Can it wait?" as she slides toward the end of the bed with the blanket wrapped around her waist. She grabs Eddie Sr. around the waist kissing on his stomach. Eddie Sr. pulls away, turns and walks to the shower. While Eddie Sr. is showering, Sheila washes her face, hands, and brushes her teeth, rushes downstairs to cook Eddie's breakfast. Eddie Sr. steps into the kitchen wearing a fresh pair of jeans and a button up shirt.

Sheila turns and looks at Eddie Sr. "Is that my Eddie? Damn! Babe, you look good this morning! You're really trimming down. And you smell nice."

Eddie Sr. replies, "I don't have time to eat breakfast."

Sheila responds, "What do you mean you don't have time to eat breakfast? Where's the race? You sure are in a hurry."

Eddie Sr. answers, "I'm not eating all that fat boy stuff anymore."

Sheila gives him a hard stare. "Well, excuse me for wanting to fix my husband's breakfast."

Eddie Sr. sarcastically, "You're excused. Put some clothes on. The boys are getting too big to see you walking around in a sheer robe."

Sheila responds, "Where are you really going this early? You on some shit again."

Eddie Sr. turns and grabs his keys from the counter, reaches in his pocket, pulls seven one hundred dollar bills out, places them on the counter. "Here's a few dollars for you and the boys to go out for breakfast, and pick up the boys some new shoes. E.J. asked me for a pair of Jordan's." Ignoring Sheila's question, Eddie Sr. leans over and kisses Sheila on the cheek, turns and walks out the front door.

Sheila blurts out loudly, "I remember a time when this hour glass body was all you needed."

Eddie Jr. walks in the kitchen half asleep, rubbing his eyes, "Mom, who are you yelling at?"

Sheila replies, "Your dad. Now go wake your brothers. We're going shopping today. E.J. runs to wake his brothers so that they could go shopping and out to breakfast.

"ROOSEVELT and VICTOR get up we're going shopping for my Jordan's." Sheila has the boys all dressed in the car, and she asks them, "Where do you guys want to eat breakfast?"

They scream out places at once, "E.J., The Pancake House." Roosevelt screams, "Man, ain't nobody trying to go there." Victor the youngest screams, "Let's go to Buns!"

Everybody starts laughing. Sheila replies, "No, Sweetie, we're going to breakfast, not lunch." Sheila puts the car in gear with a big smile on her face thinking about what her baby boy just said. She looks in the rearview mirror at Victor, "Buns, huh?"

The radio is playing in the car. Sheila drives pass Eddie Sr.'s office. His truck is in the parking lot and a new car without license plates. Sheila drives right passed as the boys look out the window at their father's office. Sheila pulls in the parking lot of one of her childhood favorites, The House of Waffles. She and the boys go inside to eat breakfast. The restaurant is packed with waiting times of fifteen minutes. Sheila is about to sit when the owner walks over to her.

"Hey Little Sheila," Mr. Thomas said.

Sheila blushes, "Hello Mr. Thomas"

Mr. Thomas looks at all the boys, "Are these your young men?"

"Yes, these are my babies, Eddie Jr., Roosevelt, and Victor."

Mr. Thomas extends his hand to shake the boys' hands.

"They sure don't act like babies. Well dressed and well mannered. You young men follow me. Your table is ready."

They followed Mr. Thomas to their booth. Mr. Thomas gives Sheila a hug before they sit down. "Be sure to tell your mom and dad that I said to stop by for lunch it's on me."

"I sure will Mr. Thomas. Thanks for getting us in."

The waitress comes over takes their order. They make small talk over the voice and chatter of plates. E.J. eating his food and chewing with his mouth open. Sheila in a low scolding voice, "BOY…CHEW WITH YOUR MOUTH CLOSE. YOU KNOW BETTER THAN TO BE STUFFING ALL THAT FOOD IN YOUR MOUTH."

Victor looks over at E.J. chewing with his mouth closed teasing E.J. because he just got in trouble.

Roosevelt is always quiet.

"Mom are we still going to the mall when we leave here?"

Sheila nods yes before speaking, "Why?"

"I want a new video game."

"Okay. We'll look at one. What do you want Victor?"

Victor ponders for a second and blurts out, "A million dollars!"

They all start laughing even Victor.

Sheila giggles, "You're definitely your father's child. A million dollars," while shaking her head no.

At Eddie's office he is sitting at the computer when a group of younger guys walk in followed by an older gentleman, Mr. Tate. Eddie stands to greet Mr. Tate extending his hand. Eddie Sr. speaks, "Wow! What brings you this way when you know you shouldn't be coming here?"

Mr. Tate replies, "Relax. I'm here to see you about a loan, but since I'm here how's my safe house holding up?"

Eddie Sr. responds, "Our safe house is just that, safe."

Mr. Tate replies, "Well, that's good to know. Now for what brought me here."

Eddie Sr. asks, "And what might that be?"

Mr. Tate answers, "Like I told you, I'm looking for some financing on my latest project."

Eddie Sr. stares at him with a hint of anger, because Mr. Tate showed up at his office unannounced with his henchmen. "Now what project would that be?"

Mr. Tate replies, "Me and my guys are going into the entertainment business. Ain't that right, Fellas?"

The guys all nod their heads never speaking a word staring at Eddie Sr. "Look, Eddie, I have all the numbers worked out. All you have to do is submit the loan application." Mr. Tate reaches over to one of the guys grabbing the folder with the application in it and hands it over to Eddie Sr. "You really turn this place around. I never thought it would look this nice. Great job Big Ed."

Eddie unfazed by the compliment responds, "So what do I get out of this deal?"

Mr. Tate smiles, "You get to live. No, I'm just kidding. You get the same fees as you do from every other customer. I mean it's just business, right?"

Eddie Sr. slightly frightened plays the hard role. "Yeah, it's just that, business."

Mr. Tate replies, "That's good to know you feel that way. Like I said earlier, my accountant prepared these papers. All you have to do is submit them and collect your fee." Mr. Tate turns toward the door, one of his guys opens it, and they turn to exit. Eddie falls back into his chair ever so nervously staring off into space. His secretary, Ms. Best, enters the office. "Mr. Fox, are you okay?"

Eddie Sr. snaps out of it. "Yes! I'm just fine. Uuumm, Ms. Best, can you see that this application makes it out first thing Monday morning?"

Ms. Best replies, "Yes, Sir. I can scan the document and send it over now. This way it will be sitting on their computer when they arrive on Monday morning."

"Okay, that will work." Eddie Sr. leans forward signing the document before he sends it over to the lenders.

"You don't look so well. Is there anything else I can get for you?"

Eddie Sr. hesitates, "No. That will be all."

Ms. Best turns and walks out of Eddie's office. Eddie Sr. watches Ms. Best butt as she switches out of his office. Eddie Sr. grabs his cell phone calling his buddy Joe. Joe answers, "What's up, Fox?"

Eddie Sr. replies, "Besides the big ass on Ms. Best man, for a woman with five kids and 50 years old, she keeps that thing tight."

Joe replies, "Man, I told you a long time ago I'd been trying to crush that."

They both laugh.

"Real talk, check this out Joe. Randy just left here."

Joe asks, "Okay. What's up?"

Eddie Sr. replies, "About some loan. He also asked how other things were going."

Joe replies, "Okay. What did you say?"

Eddie Sr. responds, "What was I supposed to say? I said everything was cool."

Joe responds, "Everything is cool. A couple more deals and we'll be rid of that guy, right?"

Eddie Sr. nods his head thinking to himself "It's never that easy, but replies to Joe differently, "Yeah, I know the sooner the better for all of us. I was just touching bases with you. I'm starting to think he wants to know which houses we're using. That wasn't part of the deal we made. I'll get back at you later."

Joe replies, "Love."

They both hang up their cell phones.

One week later at Eddie's office. Eddie Sr. is sitting at his desk crunching some numbers when Ms. Best speeds into his office with a paranoid look. Eddie looks up sensing something was wrong. "Ms. Best, what's going on?"

Ms. Best speaks softly, "The Feds are here."

The Feds walk in. Agent Cole, "Are you Mr. Eddie Fox?"

Eddie shocked to see the Feds, "Ummm Yes. What is this all about Officer?"

Agent Cole with a nasty demeanor, "I'll ask the question here you just try to answer. Arrest him."

"Stand put your hands behind your back."

Eddie livid, "What the hell am I being arrested for?"

The agents ignore Eddie's questioning.

Agent Cole smirks as if he got his man, "Take him out of here."

They drag Eddie down to the Federal Building where he is put in a room with Loan Officer Taylor from Summer Bank Incorporated.

Eddie in panic mode can't figure out what happen, "Taylor, what the hell is going on?"

Taylor in a cold sweat replies, "As if you don't know already. You had me process a loan for a Randy B. Tate. You should have told me the application was fraudulent."

Eddie Sr. puzzled, "What? How would I know the application was bogus? When he gave it to me, it was all filled out."

Taylor afraid, "Well you signed off on it. Did you or did you not?"

Eddie Sr. reluctant to answer, "I did," nodding his head in approval. It's just like any other deal we made." Eddie Sr. nods his head in disbelief, "What the fuck!"

The Feds enter the room with Agent Cole leading. "Okay, Mr. Taylor, we got it all on tape. And it was just as you said. Mr. Fox had no idea the application was fraudulent. You're both free to go for now. My guys are picking up Randy B. Tate as we speak. If I were you two guys, I wouldn't get lost. I may need you to testify for the government."

Eddie Sr. confused. "What the hell just happened? TESTIFY! Taylor, you set me up? I'm not a snitch."

Taylor giggles arrogantly, "No you're not. You're an informant. I saved your ass from a bunch of legal trouble." Officer Sand laughs, "They're all snitches."

Eddie angrily, "Is that right? We'll see about that once my lawyers get involved."

Officer Sand points to the sign on the wall.

Eddie Sr. reads the sign that's small in print.

FOR YOUR PROTECTION AND THE FEDERAL BUREAU OF INVESTIGATION EVERYTHING IN THIS ROOM IS RECORDED TO INSURE SAFETY AND JUSTICE. AT NO TIME DO YOU HAVE TO SPEAK OR CONVERSE WITH ANY LAW ENFORCEMENT AGENCY WITHOUT LEGAL REPRESENTATION. HOWEVER, SPEAKING WITHOUT COUNSEL IS SUBMISSIBLE IN THE COURT OF LAW.

"Oops! You are free to go Mr. Fox. Oh, and just for the record don't wander off," Officer Cole stated.

They both get up to leave out of the Federal Building. Before Eddie Sr. could even make it out of the Federal Building the Feds had swarmed down on Randy Tate.

At Mr. Randy Tate's condo, the Feds have apprehended him. Randy Tate sits in the back of the unmarked Federal car as his right hand man, Freeman, eases over to the car, "Randy, what's up with this?"

Randy quickly speaks, "Man, that punk ass mutha fucker, Eddie, did this. Make him pay."

Freeman replies, "Don't even trip. I got him."

Agent Green turns and yells, "Hey! Get him away from that car!"

At the Fox's home, Sheila is talking with her mother on the phone. Sheila, "Yeah, Mom, everything is going pretty smooth lately. No more staying out late. Eddie's even spending time with the kids. Huh! I don't know how long it's going to last."

Mrs. Harris' response, "You just have to give Eddie time and space. I told you he'll come around. You're a good woman, smart, pretty, and a great mother to those boys. He loves you. Just give it time."

Sheila replies, "Mom, I'm in for the long haul. I love my husband. Let me get off this phone and cook these boys some dinner."

"Okay, Baby. I love you, and give my grandsons a kiss and a hug for me."

"Will do. Love you, Mom. Bye."

Mrs. Harris replies, "Bye."

Sheila hangs up the phone and goes in the basement with the boys where they are playing video games. Sheila walks up behind them kissing and hugging them. E.J. responds, "Yuck! Come on, Mom, I'm playing the game."

Roosevelt responds, "Yeah, Mom, we're big boys now. Yuck!"

Sheila grabs Victor, "I know my baby boy wants some sugar from Mommy." Victor puckers up his lips for a kiss as Sheila holds him kissing all over his face. She puts Victor down. "What do you boys want for dinner?"

E.J. replies, "I want chicken and French fries."

Roosevelt replies, "Mom, I want pizza."

Sheila asks, "And what about you little man?"

Victor excitedly replies, "I want Buns!" They mockingly laugh at Victor's reply.

Sheila responds, "The only buns you're going to get are these." Sheila starts putting her butt in his face like she is trying to smash Victor. He's laughing pushing his mother off. Sheila laughs, "My son is a butt man. What was your dad thinking taking you to eat at Buns?"

The doorbell rings. Sheila says, "I wonder who that could be? Well, boys, let me get the door and start cooking these burgers and fries." Sheila turns and walks upstairs towards the front door. She pauses when the door knob is being turned as if someone was trying to enter. She walks to the kitchen grabbing the cordless phone. She notices someone is pulling on the back screen door. She remains quiet for a moment, but the noise from the back door is getting louder. She dials 911 then yells, "I'm calling the police. You better get away from here."

Police speaks, "What's your emergency?"

Sheila replies, "Someone is trying to break into my home."

Police asks, "Are you home alone?"

Sheila replies, "No, my sons are here with me."

Police responds, "Grab your children and go to one room and lock the door. We have dispatched a unit."

Sheila turns and runs downstairs pass the back door. The glass shatters as she passes. Sheila yells, "Oh my God!"

Police ask, "What was that noise?"

Sheila replies, "They bust the back door glass as I passed by."

Police responds, "Get your children and go into one room now." Sheila grabs the boys rushing them into the laundry room. A few minutes pass, and the police operator says, "Ma'am, there's a unit outside of your home. Go to the front door now."

Sheila gathers the boys running to the front door where the police are standing when she opens it.

Officer Brown, "Is everyone alright?"

Sheila replies, "Yes. Thank God."

Officer Brown responds, "My partner and I will take a look around the premises. You didn't happen to see who or what the person looked like did you?"

Sheila replies, "Not really. He had on a black hoody."

Officer Brown, "We'll take a look around." He turns and walks away.

Sheila's upset. "Boys, go get some clothes. We're going to grandma's house."

A knock on the door startles Sheila. A loud voice speaks, "Ma'am, are you alright?" Sheila recognizes the officer's voice walking over to open the door.

Officer Brown, "Well, we searched the backyard and alley and found no one around. I'm going to need you to sign this report that we did in fact come to your call, Ms...."

Sheila replies, "Mrs. Fox. Boys, hurry before the officers leave."

Officer Brown replies, "Well, Mrs. Fox, don't hesitate to call if someone else is creeping around. We have put an alert out for the area."

Sheila yells, "Boys, come on. We're leaving now." Sheila gets all the boys in the car, and the officer escorts her off the block. Sheila grabs her cell phone to call Eddie. The phone rings several times without an answer. E.J. asks, "Mom, what is going on?"

Sheila in tears replies, "Nothing, Baby. Everything is alright." She tries Eddie's phone again and still no answer.

At Eddie's office, his workers are still trying to figure out what the hell just happened when Eddie walks in the door with a look of concern. Ms. Best speaks, "Eddie, are you okay? I didn't know who to call when the Feds came and took you away."

Eddie replies, "I'm fine. Ms. Best, get Joe Head on the phone and forward the call back to my office."

Ms. Best, "Okay, Mr. Fox."

Eddie upset, "And the rest of you, get back to work. Everything is just fine."

Everybody walks back to their work areas. Eddie walks in his office to spot his cell phone flashing. He grabs it and looks through the caller ID to find Sheila has called seven times and five blocked calls. The speakerphone comes on. Ms. Best says, "I have Joe Head on Line One."

Eddie sits and grabs the phone. "Thanks, Mary. I have the phone. Hello!"

Joe replies, "What's up, Dawg?"

Eddie responds, "Every fucking thing. Man, the Feds picked me up."

Joe surprised, "What? What the hell are you talking about?"

Eddie replies, "I'm talking about Randy."

Joe calmly says, "Now what about Randy? Calm down."

Eddie furious, "How in the hell can you tell me to calm down when everything I worked for is at stake? Huh? Tell me. You know I'm not in this by myself."

Joe angrily states, "Look, if the Feds let you go, they don't know anything."

Eddie replies, "They know I had some bogus taxes filed for him."

Joe responds, "Taxes! Man, meet me at Heaven on Seven at six o'clock."

Eddie replies, "Naw, that's not happening. I'll get up with you tomorrow. Later."

Joe disappointed, "Yeah, whenever. Peace."

Eddie hangs up the phone and calls Sheila immediately. Sheila answers, "Where the hell are you?"

Eddie tries to explain, "Honey! Please just listen for a moment. I just got out of jail."

Sheila angry, "And somebody tried to break in the house while me and the kids were there."

Eddie pauses, "What?"

Sheila replies, "Yeah! While you out there trying to play house with some other bitch, somebody was trying to break in your house!"

Eddie responds, "Where are you and the kids now?"

Sheila sarcastically, "Don't try to act all concerned about us now. We're at my mother's."

Eddie angry, "Alright. I'm on my way." He hangs up the phone and storms out of his office rushing pass Ms. Best.

Ms. Best concerned, "Mr. Fox is everything okay?"

Eddie pauses, "Tell everyone to close out the deals they have and go home."

Ms. Best stands up to talk, and Eddie turns away, walks out the door to his truck. Eddie jumps in, starts the truck looking all around before pulling off afraid he may be followed. He speeds away headed towards the Harris's home.

At Sheila's parent's home, Sheila is a nervous wreck sitting with her Mom. Mrs. Harris empathically concerned, "Sheila, listen to your mother. I know right now, Sweetie, you're hurt, but jumping all over Eddie isn't going to help your current situation."

E.J. enters the room, "Mom, can we have some money for the ice cream truck?"

Sheila snaps, "No! Don't you see me and your grandmother in here talking? Don't you see that? Look at me, boy, when I'm talking to you!"

Mrs. Harris bothered by what she just saw, "E.J., go in there and grab granny's purse and bring me a beer out of the frig." E.J. just stands there.

Sheila, "Don't stand there looking all stupid. Go do what your grandmother asked." E.J. walks off sadly.

Mrs. Harris responds in a bitter tone, "Let me tell you something. Those boys haven't did anything wrong. Whatever your problem is those boys have nothing to do with it. You understand me? I'm talking to you now. Don't sit there looking stupid say something." Sheila thinking of how her mother just made her feel drops her head in her hands.

E.J. walks back in the room with his granny's purse and beer looking at his mother, "Here you go, grandma."

Sheila picks her head up looking at E.J. extends her arms for E.J. "Come here, baby!" E.J. walks over with arms extended reaching for his mother. They hug and E.J. starts crying. Mrs. Harris gets up and walks over and they have a group hug. Eddie Sr. enters the room while everyone is in tears.

Eddie surprised, "What the hell is going on? Did somebody just die?"

Mrs. Harris replies, "No, Eddie, we just love one another so much it hurts sometimes to see people you love get hurt."

Eddie looking dumbfounded, "Sheila, we need to talk."

Mrs. Harris grabs E.J.'s hand, "Come on, E.J. Let your parents talk. Let's get some ice cream." They exit the room.

Eddie starts tearing, "I'm sorry … I'm sorry … I'll tell you everything that's going on. I'm sorry!" Eddie fights back his tears and sits Sheila down to explain to her what has been happening. Eddie and Sheila both take a seat right next to one another. Eddie looks deep into Sheila's eyes to explain, "Sheila, I am deeply sorry for everything that has gone on today. The Feds came and took me out of my office for some business deals I made for a friend. Now my thought is the guy I did the deal with sent someone to look for me and that's why they came to the house."

Sheila responds, "Because you made a bad deal? That doesn't make any sense."

Eddie exclaims, "No, because the Feds tricked me into telling on this drug dealer I know named Randy. The problem is Randy got picked up by the Feds as well."

Sheila replies, "Were drugs involved with the deal?"

Eddie replies, "No, but I've put away some money for this guy, and I think he may think I'm trying to keep it."

Sheila surprised, "How much money did you endanger your family for? Eddie?"

Eddie responds, "A lot but never to put you all in harm's way. In fact we're moving to a much better community. I was going to surprise you with it for our anniversary, but we can move in as soon as possible."

Sheila stares at Eddie, "So you're telling me this is where all the extra money has been coming from? Randy?"

Eddie replies, "No. Business isn't bad although Randy's given me quite an amount of cash."

Sheila slides away from Eddie slightly, "So you're saying all those nights you didn't come home you were doing business with Randy, and there's no other woman?"

Eddie looks Sheila right in her eyes, "No, there's no other woman. I love you, Sheila Fox."

In the kitchen, Grandma Harris is holding E.J. as she sits at the table with Granddad Harris.

Granddad, "Why are you holding onto that boy? He ain't no baby."

Grandma Harris holds him, "He's grandma's baby."

The little brother, Victor, walks into the kitchen. "Man! E.J., you made us miss the ice cream truck. It's at the end of the block. Why you all hugged up under grandma like a little girl?"

Granddad Harris starts laughing, "I told your grandma she's babying him like a little girl. Vic, do granddad a favor and hand me one of those beers out the frig." Vic opens the refrigerator, grabs a beer, closes the frig, walks the beer to granddad. Granddad Harris smiles as he cracks open the can taking a sip, "Ahh! Thanks Vic."

Victor exclaims, "E.J., you coming back outside or you staying in the house like a little baby?"

Granddad replies, "More like a little girl up in here crying about nothing."

Grandma Harris, "Alright, James, that's enough. This boy has been through enough today. Now go out on the front with your Uncle Reggie. I know it's late, but the ice cream truck will come back around." E.J. jumps up running toward Victor. Victor takes off running screaming, "UNCLE REGGIE … E.J. GONNA HIT ME." As they both ran out the front door.

Back in the bedroom Sheila is upset talking with Eddie Sr. "Ed, I'm not going back to that house. You can have your friends or whoever moves our things to the new house. I refuse to go back to that house with my kids."

Eddie takes a deep breathe, "Okay. I'll work on it."

Sheila says with a serious attitude, "This better not be about you and some bitch you're messing around with. I swear."

Ed uneasy about the incident, "It's not. I promise you that." He reaches for Sheila trying to pull her close to him. She pulls away storming out of the room. He just sits pondering his next move.

A couple of weeks have passed and Sheila is still living with her parents. It's morning and she gets up to prepare breakfast for the boys. She walks in the kitchen in a tank top and some short shorts to find Bryant sitting at the kitchen table. Sheila caught off guard slightly irritated, "DAMN! Do you live here or what?"

Bryant stares at her with a fake laugh, "Ha ha! That's funny. I'm waiting on Reggie, and good morning to you Ms. Thang!" Sheila walks over to the cabinet bends down to grab a pot. Bryant leans forward in his seat to catch an eye full of Sheila's ass, "Nice buns hun!"

Sheila immediately stands up laughing looking at Bryant. She smirks placing one hand on her hip, hearing him say that made her think of Victor. "That is so lame. You sound like my five year old son. Talking about nice buns, get a life."

"I bet your five year old son can't work them buns the way I can," Bryant responded.

Sheila's nipples got erect through her tank top. She quickly turns away, "I hope he doesn't know anything about working some buns at five years old. Or should I say he knows more than you at five, Ha!"

Reggie walks in the kitchen smacking Bryant on the head lightly, "Come on youngster it's time to get it crackin'."

Bryant stands up, "MAN! Bro, I told you about putting your paws on me."

Reggie playfully, "Yeah, okay Dawg. Let's ride."

Reggie walks in front of Bryant. Bryant looks over at Sheila rolling his tongue in a slow circular motion and whisper, "Get with me."

Sheila grins with her arms crossed over her breast covering her nipples. Victor comes running into the kitchen with his arms in the air, "MOMMIE!!"

Bryant exits the kitchen as Sheila reaches down to pick up Victor. "HEY! Lil man. How is mommy's baby boy?"

"I'm fine Mommy," Grabbing her around the neck and kissing her on the cheek.

She hugs him tightly. "So where are your brothers?"

"In the room playing the game." Victor said.

"What? I dare those boys to be playing games this time of morning." Sheila heads toward the bedroom with Victor on her heels.

"Mommy! They won't let me play," Victor said.

"Oh! They'll let you play. E.J. and Roosevelt TURN THAT GAME OFF NOW! Come on in here for breakfast." She startles them as the room door opens E.J. and Roosevelt are sitting in the middle of the floor playing the game. They both appear surprised. "GET UP!" Sheila yelled.

"I told you about not letting my baby play. Turn it off and go wash your hands for breakfast."

E.J. starts to turn the game off.

Sheila yells "Leave it on!" She grabs the controller passing it to Victor, "Here baby." Victor's face lights up as he grabs the controller. E.J. and Roosevelt both pout on their way out of the room.

E.J. frowns as they walked out the door.

"Victor a snitch he always tells on us."

Sheila overheard what E.J. said about Victor.

"E.J., bring your ass right here and right now."

E.J. drops his head and walks back over to his mom.

"Yes."

Sheila looks down at E.J. "Look at me when I'm talking to you."

E.J. lifts his head up.

"Let's get this straight. There are no snitches in this family. Don't call Victor or anyone else in this family a snitch. Do you understand me?"

E.J. nods in agreement.

"I can't hear you."

"Yes mom."

"Now go in there and eat some breakfast before I whip your behind."

E.J. drops his head and walks away.

"And pick your head up. Victor cut that game off now go eat breakfast. Stop telling all the damn time you talk too much." E.J. heard his mom scolding Victor he stops, turn around and teases Victor silently. Victor sticks his tongue out at E.J. Sheila turns around catches E.J. making faces. Sheila shakes her head.

Two weeks later. The Fox Family is moving in their new single family home in a middle class gated community with vaulted ceilings, open entry way, loft, large kitchen, breakfast nook, morning room, family room, office, library, five bedrooms, mother-in-law suite, three and a half baths, three car garage with a drive-way roundabout in the front area of the house. Sheila is very excited as family and friends help them move. Eddie Sr. stands watching Reggie and Bryant move a very expensive couch hoping that they don't damage it. Sheila places her box down putting her hands on her hip, "Ed! What's wrong?"

Sheila's nieces Tonya and Shanae continue to carry boxes in the house walking pass Eddie Sr.

"Nothing. What prompt you to ask me that?" Eddie Sr. responded.

Sheila sarcastically, "That crazy ass look on your face. That's what and you're staring in my niece's direction."

Tonya stops in the doorway where Eddie and Sheila are standing to the side of them.

"Auntie Sheila, which room does this box go in, it's not marked?" Tonya asked.

"OH MY GOD! It's right there Tonya. Kids room, and how did you come to help in those tight ass jeans. Your butt is too big for those jeans," Sheila responded.

Tonya looks back at her butt while holding the box. "I thought that I might meet one of Ed's rich friends," as she glances over at Eddie.

Eddie nervously moves quickly, "Well, let's get it cracking it's getting late." Reggie picks up his pace grabbing two or three boxes at a time. Shanae is helping Auntie Sheila with her clothes. Tonya and Bryant are taking a water break checking their cell phones. Tonya admires the house looking all around. She goes into the master bedroom where Shanae and Auntie Sheila are hanging up clothes.

"Auntie this is a very nice house. Five bedrooms with a three car garage and full finished basement. Wow! Eddie really *turnt* the game up with this one," Tonya said.

"Yes, he did the damn thang. It's a long way from a three bedroom house in the hood," Sheila replied.

Tonya sips on her water looking around the room.

"Damn Tonya, you going to help or what?" Shanae asked.

"Girl! I just got my nails done. I'm not trying to break one," Tonya exclaimed.

Shanae irritated, "What the hell you come for if you didn't want to help. You're the most irritating."

Auntie Sheila cuts them off before they can even get started. "Okay, let's go back downstairs. Everyone is tired. Come on."

The night has fallen and everything has been moved inside the house. Eddie orders pizza and grabs some beer for the guys.

"I'm glad the movers will bring everything else. I'm beat," Eddie Sr. said.

Reggie yarns! "Well Sis, it's time for me to get back to the hood."

"Yeah! A brother gotta check that dough?" Bryant added.

Shanae frowns at Bryant, "What dough you talking about? Cookie dough because you ain't got no money."

Everyone in the room laughs.

"You're gonna stop trying to put a brother on clown status!" Bryant said slightly irritated.

Shanae gives Bryant the once over look, "No I am not."

Everyone continues to laugh.

"You know I love you like a bald head stepchild." Shanae added to the insult.

Eddie in tears with laughter, "Woo … Shanae … girl … you don't have one ounce of sense."

Bryant upset, "Shanae, you going to stop trying to treat me like a goofy."

Eddie cuts the conversation off quickly before it becomes too personal. "Damn yawl crazy. I haven't laughed that hard in quite some time. Anyway on behalf of me and my family, we thank you all for your help." Eddie walks over to Reggie and shakes his hand in appreciation sliding a hundred dollar bill in his hand.

"Thanks Brother!" Eddie said.

"It's not a problem," Reggie responded.

Tonya with a big grin, "It was our pleasure to help the family. Who knows maybe one day you'll be helping one of us move into our own place."

Sheila smiles, "Yeah! Thanks for coming out and good night."

"Dang Auntie! You just going to put us out like that?" Shanae asked. "I know you want to consecrate this house, but dang!"

Tonya gives Shanae that she is stupid look, "It's not consecrate. It's consummate."

"NO! It's consecrate, to make sacred. You're not the only person in this family that could have gone to law school." Shanae said.

Tonya ponders, "Yeah whatever! I still think I'm right."

"Regardless, it's about to go down. Bye, bye!" Sheila said as she walks them toward the door.

Bryant starts out the door, "Shit was about to get thick up in here. I love cat fights."

Sheila very witty, "I just bet you do. Seeing how you never get any cat!"

Everyone erupts in laughter as they walk out the door.

Eddie stands in the doorway shaking his head as they all pull off.

Sheila has a puzzled look on her face when Eddie turns around.

"What's going on in that head of yours?" Eddie asked.

Sheila answers, "Tonya's new car. I've seen that car somewhere before. I just can't place where it was. And where is Joe? Why didn't he come to help out?"

"With all that's going on, we need to keep a little distance between us."

"Oh okay, that makes sense."

Eddie grabs Sheila around her waist turning her toward him. He leans down to kiss her. They share a very passionate kiss.

Sheila in a soft voice, "I love our new home."

Eddie palms her butt with both hands and whispers in her ear, "Are we going to consecrate or consummate our home?"

"You're so silly! I don't want to debate about which is the right word," Sheila responded. She pulls away from Eddie's grip undressing leaving a trail of clothes for him to follow. Eddie Sr. picks up every stitch of clothing following her trail. He reaches the room and Sheila is standing there in her matching lace bra and thong set. Eddie sits on the bed pulling Sheila close kissing her stomach. Sheila a little insecure about her stomach pulls away from him removing her bra. She heads for the shower. Eddie sits admiring that voluptuous butt that's firm as the day he met her. He follows her to the shower where the steam from the water has fogged the room. He removes his clothes dims the lights before opening the shower door. Sheila caramel colored skin glisten as the water runs down her breast. Eddie slowly gets in extending his hand for the body sponge. He gently washes Sheila up moving down to her lower back. Sheila arches her back leaning forward placing her arms on the wall. Eddie drops the sponge grabbing her hips as he inserts himself inside of her. Sheila moans as Eddie thrust deep inside of her. The more Sheila moans the more turned on Eddie became. As the water ran down Eddie's back he began to think about how he wanted this moment to last. He pulls Sheila up squeezing her breast as he moves slowly in and out of her wetness. The water splashes against their bodies as she backs up on Eddie with force. Sheila pulls away from Eddie grabbing her hair and wrapping it up in a ponytail. Eddie lifts Sheila up pinning her to the shower wall with her legs wrapped around his waist. She places her hands on Eddie's broad shoulders as he continues to penetrate with light slow strokes.

The next day Sheila is at home unpacking boxes. She starts in the kids' room working her way to the living-room. After about five hours of non-stop cleaning and unpacking she takes a seat in the kitchen. She sits at the table eating grapes. She grabs her cell phone calling her mom. "Hey mom!"

"Hey Sweetie! How's the new house coming along?"

"It's cool mom."

"What's wrong? I can hear it in your voice."

"Nothing."

"You know that Eddie is a great father and good provider, right? Remember Sheila all relationships have problems. It's more about how you work through them that counts." Momma Jean said.

"Yes, ma'am. I know mom. All those late nights just keep playing over in my mind. I'm good I just wanted to hear your voice. Love you!"

"Love you too Sheila. You can leave the boys over as long as you like."

"Okay Mom. Thanks. Bye!"

"Bye baby."

"Mom, I was thinking that I should come," The phone goes dead Sheila's mother had hung up before she could finish what she was saying. Sheila takes a look around the kitchen looking at more boxes she gets irritated feeling overwhelmed. Sheila speaking out loud to herself, "*Dammit! I haven't made any real progress.*" She leans forward resting her head in the palm of her hands in disgust.

Eddie is back up to his old tricks hanging out late with the fellas shooting dice. His good friend Joe is hosting a crap game at his home. Joe has a topnotch bachelor pad. His basement has a big screen T.V. with surround sound and a nice pool table that they use to shoot dice on. Joe is standing next to Eddie Sr. when he is shooting the dice.

Joe upset, "Damn Big Papa. You been tearing us a new ass hole around here. It doesn't pay to fade your bet lucky ass Dude. I'm jumping on the side bet. Somebody fade this Dude."

Eddie Sr. smiles slightly scooping up the dice from the table, "Yeah! Man when it's good it's all good."

Big Mike Chuckles, "Yeah, and when it's all bad it's all bad too. Five hundred you don't pass."

Big Mike was one of the infamous drug-boys in the city. Big Mike was very smooth and had crew on lock. They were getting money hand over fist.

Eddie Sr. smirks, "Bet a stack I do pass?"

Big Mike grins, "Bet it!" Throwing the money down on the table, "I spend more money than that on my shoes." Big Mike one of the sharpest dressed hustlers in the city has a lot of power and money to go along with it.

Eddie Sr. grabs the dice shakes them in his hand, "Hit'em and quit'em!" He scoops the dice up and quickly shakes and roll again, "Hit'em and…." One of the dice spins and stops on Eddie's point. Eddie Sr. snaps his finger, "QUIT'EM!"

Joe pissed he lost his large side bet, "SHIT! This lucky son of gun."

Eddie smiles from ear to ear, "Well, fellas I got to roll."

"You damn right it's your roll." Old Man Baker stated. OMB a gangster to the tenth power was one of the city's most notorious men.

Eddie. Sr. looks up at OMB as he stacks his cash up, "Naw, I'm done homie."

OMB angry, "Like hell! You've been winning for the last two weeks. It's time you let us win some of our money back.

Eddie Sr. defensive, "Bullshit! What about when I lost for two straight months? I didn't hear anybody saying shit then. Fuck that I'm gone."

Attitudes start to build. Joe stops the beef, "Hey Fella's. This is supposed to be a friendly game. If you can't handle losing it, don't bet it. On the real, if he wants out it's his choice to leave cash on the table. There's plenty of money in this room left."

Big Mike opens a small man bag full of cash, "Yo! Let the working man get on. Pass the mother fucking dice."

OMB felt challenged as Eddie passed the dice to him, "This ain't over you about fifteen stacks up on me. If you're quitting pay back my cash now."

Eddie stares with a look that could kill, "If you want it get it like Tyson."

Big Mike, Joe, Sherman, and Black look at Eddie like he lost his fucking mind.

OMB throws two racks on the table waiting to be faded looking in Eddie Sr.'s direction. Big Mike throws two racks on the table fading the bet. Eddie counts up his cash placing it into his pouch. OMB grits his teeth then rolls the dice and looks up at Eddie. "Like Tyson huh?"

Eddie didn't even respond just turned and walked out the door. Eddie quickly gets in his car speeding away looking in the rearview mirrors.

Sheila had finished cleaning up the house for the day. She decided to wind down with a nice hot bath and drink. She enters the master bedroom bathroom stopping at the double sink looking at the granite top. She opens the cabinet grabbing a ponytail holder. She pulls her hair up as she brushes it flat to put the ponytail holder on. Sheila's hair is beautiful, thick and hangs to below her shoulders. She applies some facial cream turns to run the water in the Jacuzzi style tub. While the water is running Sheila runs downstairs to grab a bottle of wine and cell phone. The bathroom was equipped with Bluetooth technology so Sheila turns on the slow jams. The tub is ready and so is Sheila as she turns on the motor in the tub. Dimming the lights she removes her clothes thinking that Eddie could come in at any moment. Sheila eases into the tub not wanting to slip. She places her drink and cell phone at the end of the tub. The water is just the right temperature as she leans back against the jets. She sips on her drink and close her eyes while listening to the music.

She sits up in the tub refills her glass reminiscing as she sips on her drink. Before long the water has turned cold and she had drank too much. A little tipsy she steps out of the tub drying off. As she walks over to the full-length mirror she looks at her cell phone on the counter. She picks it up to call Eddie Sr. instead she changes the music and pours another drink. While listening to music she puts on her make-up and pulls her hair down.

She looks in the mirror at her lipstick speaking out loud, "Girl those lips are popping!" She continues to get dressed with a matching Vicki Secret boy-shorts and bra set. She checks out herself in the mirror grabs her cell phone takes a selfie photo. She then heads to the bedroom where she polishes her toes light pink. She puts on a sheer robe expecting Eddie Sr. to come in at any moment. She rushes down to the living-room waiting on Eddie Sr. to walk in at any moment. While waiting on Eddie Sr., she pulls a novel out of her over-sized purse "The Party Girl." She begins reading until she falls asleep. Eddie Sr. comes in just before sun up to find her sleeping on the couch with an empty bottle of wine and novel beside her. He grabs a blanket to cover her and proceeds upstairs to the shower. After his shower Eddie Sr. sat on the end of the bed counting his money. He counts out twenty-one thousand. He smirks, thinking about all the money he had lost over the last couple of months. He places the money back in the bag and went to sleep in the bedroom. Sheila awakes by the loud sound of the doorbell, DING DONG, DING DONG!

Instantly she realizes that the kids were scheduled to come home this morning. She rushes up to the bedroom to find Eddie Sr. sitting on the end of the bed. "Who the hell is that this time of morning?" Eddie Sr. asked.

She slides her clothes on, "That's Shanae and the boys." She glances over at the clock 10:30 a.m. "And what time did you get in?" Sheila asked.

Eddie Sr. ignores Sheila's question, "Damn, I got to get to work."

"Ed, I didn't marry you to be a single parent."

Eddie Sr. rushes into the bathroom preparing to leave without saying a word.

Sheila with an attitude, "WELL, hell I didn't." She walks out the room down to the front door. She opens the front door to find Shanae and the boys standing there.

"Dang! Auntie Sheila, I thought you were going to let us freeze out here." Shanae said.

Sheila slightly irritated forces a smile, "Hey boys!"

Three boys in unison speak back, "HEY MOMMIE!" and embrace her with hugs.

"Girl please! You're my favorite niece. I would never leave you out in the cold. Boys go to the back room I have your game set up for you."

The kids take off running to the back room.

"So how was the first week in your new house? I see you been getting it in because, those lips are poppin'!" Shanae stated.

Sheila frowns, "These lips are the only thing poppin' around here."

Shanae laughs, "Auntie you're crazy."

"Eddie's back up to his same old tricks. No Eddie." Sheila said.

Shanae sits on the couch in disbelief," You kidding me right?"

"I wish that I was kidding. I'm serious girl no Eddie yesterday or last night, but his black ass up there now." Tears start to form in Sheila's eyes. "Girl I got to get something for this headache," as she rushes off. Eddie comes down the stairs wearing a nice pair of slacks and sweater smelling fresh. "I'm gone! Hey Shanae, thanks for watching the boys." He grabs his keys from the table walks out the door.

Shanae trying to accommodate her aunt yells, "If you need me I'll be in the back with the boys."

Sheila yells, "Make yourself at home."

Shanae makes her way back to the room with the boys to play this virtual game D.R.O.N.E.

E.J. shouting as Shanae enters the room, "Take that!"

"Roosevelt, let me get him?" Shanae asks as she took a seat next to Roosevelt.

Roosevelt always mild mannered, "Get Him cousin Nae!"

Shanae moving quickly throughout level one catches E.J. on level two.

Victor covers his eyes, "Watch out cousin Nae-nae!"

Shanae maneuvers pass the object and beats E.J. to the next level.

"Wow! Nae-nae, you beat E.J.," exclaimed Roosevelt.

E.J. drops his controller, "I was tired anyway."

Victor excited grabs the controller, "Cousin Nae can I play?"

"You sure can," with a big grin, Shanae answered.

E.J. walks off to his mother's room. He knocks on the door before entering.

KNOCK KNOCK!!! E.J. enters the room.

"Who is it? Well, if you were just going to walk in why knock?" Sheila yelled.

E.J. looks over at his mom and hunches his shoulders, "Mom, I wanted to ask you something?" He tries to remember what it is he wanted to ask, "Ummm! Oh yeah! Why was cousin Tonya's car at Dad's job?"

Sheila caught off guard, "WHAT? Why would you think that was cousin Tonya's car E.J.?"

E.J. smiles playfully, "Mom, because I like cars. You never remember anything. Remember the day you took us shopping and to breakfast?"

"Yes. What about that day E.J."

"Cousin Tonya's car was parked in the lot when we drove pass Dad's office. Remember Mom?" E.J. asked excitedly.

Sheila sits on the edge of the bed thinking hard about the day.

"Yes E.J., I do remember the red car out there. But there are plenty cars out there red and look like that model."

E.J. unable to comprehend the seriousness of the situation playful, "Duh! I know that mom, because cousin Tonya is the only one I seen with those rims at Grandma's house and Dad's job."

Sheila's heart sank in her chest thinking about the possibility. She reaches for E.J., "Come here baby."

She grabs E.J. looks him in his eyes, "Don't say anything about what you've seen. Okay?"

E.J. stares in his mom's eyes confused and frightened, "Okay Mom. Did I do something wrong?"

His eyes start to water as he looks at the sadness in his mom's eyes. She pulls him to her hugging him tightly. E.J. starts to cry.

"Sshhhh!!" She starts to rock E.J. back and forth as the tears stream down her cheeks.

"It's okay. I love you don't forget that." Sheila told E.J. kissing his forehead.

Shanae walks in the room and observes, "What the … is going on in here? What's wrong with E.J. why is he crying?"

"Nothing is wrong. We're good." Sheila said holding back her tears.

"He just love his momma." Sheila said.

"Auntie Sheila something is wrong." Shanae stated.

"E.J. go play with your brothers." Sheila implied.

E.J. wipes his eyes, leaves the room to return downstairs.

Sheila sits on the end of the bed rocking wiping away her tears.

Shanae with a great deal of concern pleads, "Auntie Sheila what's wrong?"

"Nothing Nae. I'm fine. Just tired of the B.S...." Sheila stated.

Shanae getting upset eyes got watery," I'm going to call Grandma. Tell me?"

Sheila stops crying takes a deep breath and exhale, "No need to call Momma, I'm fine. Just go down to the bar and bring me a wine cooler, so I can get rid of this damn headache."

Later on that evening, Eddie Sr. is at a restaurant with some interns from Tonya's school. Tonya and her friends all attend Loyola University. Meeting at Nikki's was convenient for Eddie Sr. and the ladies it was the mid-point for travel. Nikki's Soul Food Palace, Nikki's restaurant was well known for its mac & cheese, cabbage, fried chicken and peach cobbler. Just outside of the West Loop the restaurant stay packed small in size, but big in business. The décor was that of many celebrities who had eaten there. The waiting time for dining was always 30 minutes or more. You could smell the food in the streets if you drove by.

The five of them are sitting in a booth with Tonya sitting right next to Eddie Sr. All of the young ladies are very attractive and law students studying real estate, criminal, sports management, and business law. Tonya has her hand on Eddie's knee under the table. They're sharing small talk about ideas and drinking alcohol. Eddie stops the waiter, "Sir don't let anybody's glass get empty. Keep the drinks coming." He reaches in his pocket handing the waiter his black card.

"Yes Sir," The waiter answered reaching for the black card.

Tonya cannot keep her lustful eyes off Eddie. The other girls notice something strange. Tonya a little tipsy places her hand under the table touching Eddie's thigh. "Eddie, tell them about the market." Tonya requested as her hand move up his thigh.

Eddie reaches under the table removing Tonya's hand off his leg.

"Like, I was about to say, 'The housing market isn't what one would hope to see.'" Eddie stated.

Kim a very intelligent and attractive professional woman questions Eddie's theory on the market.

"So you telling me the market currently is bad for everyone?" Kim asked.

Tonya's expression hung on to Eddie's every word.

"No, what I am saying is that it's a buyer's market." Eddie answered.

Sabrina an entertainment law student nerd type, very reserved, and cute asked, "Elaborate on the buyer's market for me a little?"

"What I mean. Is the only people looking to buy property at this time would be investors. Those who can afford to sit on the property until the market recovers or develop the property that was purchased for a profit." Eddie stated.

Everybody sips on their drinks as Eddie broke down the language. They all nodded in agreement with Eddie as he broke it down.

Tonya one too many drinks, "Girls, he looks like a Big old Teddy Bear, right?"

The entire table looks in Eddie's direction. He quickly jumps up removing Tonya's hand once again off his leg reaching into his pocket pulling a stack of cash. "WAITER!" Eddie shouted.

"Well, Ladies it's been nice meeting you all, but it's time I get home to my family." Eddie said looking directly at Tonya.

Tonya with lust in her eyes, "Boo it's still early." She checks the time on her watch. The waiter walks up, "Yes Sir?"

"I'll be paying cash. What's my damage on that bill?"

Eddie tosses three hundred dollar bills on the table "That should cover the bill. It's nice to have met you all." He places his black card back into his wallet.

"On behalf of me and my friends we thank you Uncle Eddie. It was nice of you to take time out of your busy schedule for me. I mean us." Tonya said sarcastically.

Kim extends her hand to Eddie. "Pleasure to have met you as well."

"Likewise." Eddie replied shaking Kim's hand.

Sharon shares Kim sentiment. "Thank you!"

Sabrina the flirty girl out of the group extends her hand holding Eddie's tightly, "Thanks for dinner and a great conversation. It's rare you find looks, smarts, manners, and money in one man. Your wife is a lucky girl."

Eddie smirks. "Thanks. Sabrina you're right my wife is a lucky woman."

"Yes, yes...." Sabrina stated.

"Have a good evening everyone." Eddie turns and walks away.

Sharon cheesing up a storm, "Damn, that's one smooth brother right there. He's such a gentleman. He is a little bigger than I'm used to but I'll make it work."

Kim nodding in agreement, "You said a mouth full with that being said."

"Yeah! I bet he's more than a mouth full." Sabrina said.

They all laugh at once.

Tonya with a smirk on her face, "Who you telling?"

Sabrina gives Tonya a hard stare, "Bitch, I know you not messing with your Auntie's husband? Your uncle?"

Kim looks at Tonya's facial expression, "You Bitch! I know you're not?"

Tonya grins, "If I was, what business would that be of yours?"

Sharon falls back in her seat, "Your Auntie is going to be devastated!"

Tonya unfazed by their remarks rolls her eyes, "Oh well. She'll never find out."

Kim curious about Eddie, "Okay, spill the beans. Is he packing?"

"A minute ago you were all an ass about the situation. Now Bitch you want details. I don't think so." Tonya said sipping on the last of her drink.

"Tonya it's your Auntie's husband, your uncle!" Sharon exclaimed.

"Bitch please! Not you. I know you're not the one to talk. Ms. I take it up the ass ain't cheating. Now you want to pass judgment? I think not!" Tonya responded.

Sabrina surprised, "OMG! WHAT THE HELL KIM?"

Sharon frowns with great disappointment, "You bitches are skank nasty."

Tonya with no shame, "Okay, since you all want to know. I'm going to put it out there."

The table goes silent and they all focus on Tonya.

Tonya with a very serious look on her face grins then speaks, "Hell yeah he packing. It's long, black and crooked at the end."

They all are stunned by Tonya's comments.

"Woo! You are too much Tonya," Sabrina said.

Kim laughing, "You gave *keeping it real* a new meaning."

Sharon slightly embarrassed mouth hung open, "Tonya! Girl you and your stories, so you're not really fucking him right?"

The table goes silent again as they all stare at Kim.

"Why is this Bitch hair black when she's a true Blonde? Yes I'm fucking him, that's my Captain hook." Tonya said.

The table erupts in laughter except Kim as she shakes her head in disbelief. Tears are in Sabrina's eyes from laughing so hard, "I can't wait to get hooked!"

They burst out laughing again this time Sharon had to join the laughter.

They calm down wiping tears from their eyes and Sharon speaks.

"Sshhh! really Tonya, you know you Bogus!" Sharon stated.

"In your ass Sharon!" Tonya blurted.

The table erupts in laughter again.

"Anal Sharon really?" Kim asked.

Later on that evening Eddie walks in the bedroom to find Shanae and Sheila talking. He pauses in his tracks when he notices sadness in the room. Shanae is consoling Sheila by rubbing her back. Eddie slightly worried eases over to the dresser drawer putting money in his desk. Sheila lifts her head looking in Eddie Sr.'s direction wiping her tears away.

"What's happening? Why are you crying?" Eddie Sr. asked.

"I'm not crying." Sheila responded.

Eddie moves closers to Sheila. "What's the problem?"

Shanae looks at Eddie Sr. as if she could kill him. Eddie pays her hardly any attention.

"I don't know why you giving me the evil eye." Eddie Sr. stated.

Shanae had been there the entire day with her Auntie Sheila. They cooked lunch for the boys and returned to the bedroom to talk.

"If you need me Auntie, call me. I'll take the kids back with me. You are coming to Momma's house, right?" Shanae asked.

Eddie Sr. getting annoyed, "Is someone gonna tell me what's going on?"

Sheila responds, "Nothing dammit!"

"OKAY! Shanae don't leave on my account." Eddie Sr. said.

Shanae rolls her eyes at Eddie Sr., "Oh I'm not. Believe that!"

She stares Eddie Sr. up and down. "Later Auntie, I got to go pick up my kids from their Dad. I'll see you later." She walks over and gives Sheila a hug and kiss on the cheek before walking out of the room and heads for the front door. Eddie walks over in front of

Sheila, "So are you going to tell me what's going on or naw?" Eddie Sr. asked.

Sheila picks up her drink sips it and calmly speaks, "Nothing!"

Eddie Sr. starts to undress a little upset about the lack of communication. He heads for the shower wearing his boxer briefs. He doubles back to the room grabbing clean underclothing. Sheila jumps up off the bed following him to the shower. Eddie Sr. turns to find Sheila all up on him. He smirks, "Why you following me around like a lost puppy?"

Sheila takes a deep breathe, "First stop yelling. I don't want the boys to think we're fighting."

"You think they can hear us from your mom's house. Shanae took the boys."

"She didn't take them. There still here. Oh, so you think I'm a puppy huh?"

Eddie Sr. looks Sheila square in her eyes," No, Sweetheart you're my wife. And I expect for you to keep it real with me at all times."

Sheila whispers in a low sexy voice, "Is that how you do?"

Sheila slides Eddie's boxers off then removes her shirt. She kneels down in front of him. Sheila removes her bra sliding her arms out. She growls as if she is a puppy.

Eddie Sr. giggles, "What are you doing?"

Sheila seductively speaks, "I'm your puppy, right?"

She licks his inner thigh. Eddie Sr. closes his eyes enjoying the moment. She continues to lick around his manhood and starts sniffing his penis as if she was a dog. Eddie Sr. opens his eyes looking down at Sheila.

Sheila growls loud holding his penis in her hand. Eddie has a full erection. She continues to toy with Eddie taking one big sniff then taking Eddie deep inside her mouth. Eddie Sr. knees buckle slightly as she sucks long and hard. Eddie grabs the back of her head for balance and control. He pulls her up removing the rest of her clothing sliding her thong off. They both step inside the shower. Sheila stands under the showerhead as the water runs down her back. Eddie slides behind her blocking the water. He grabs the body sponge and begins to wash Sheila's back. Sheila knocks the sponge out of Eddie's hand. She arches her back bending over slightly. Eddie grabs her around her waist and enters her wetness. Sheila moans, "Ahhh!"

The water splashes off Eddie's back as he strokes Sheila with long slow strokes. Her hands are against the back of the shower as she pushes back on Eddie.

She moans louder looking back at Eddie, "AHHH!!!"

Eddie Sr. reaches behind him turning off the water. The shower is steamy he spins her around kissing her before carrying her to the bed. He lays her back on the bed standing over her. He spreads her legs apart. She lays there in anticipation. He kneels down licking her clitoral. She begins breathing heavily as Eddie Sr. stimulates her clit.

"Ohhhh!!! Shit! Ohhh!!!! Shit!!! That feels good!" Sheila repeated.

At that moment Eddie glances at Sheila but has a vision of Tonya. He rotates his tongue in a circular motion driving Sheila crazy. "OOHHH…AHHHH… I LOVE THIS…I LOVE YOU…..OOOH!! AHH!!!!!!!!" Her body tenses up as she tries to pull away from Eddie's grip. Eddie climbs up in the bed pulling Sheila on top of him. She rides him slowly as he squeezes her breast.

"Dammit Girl!!!!" Eddie Sr. blurts out. Sheila throws her hair back and sits straight up on Eddie. A little pain mixed with a lot of pleasure Sheila thought bending back forward grinding down on Eddie. He dismounts Sheila. She lies on her side with him right behind her. Eddie places one of her legs on top of his thigh as he penetrates from the side. He slides his hand between her legs gently massages her clit. Sheila moans out as he takes short stokes and slight pressure on her clit. Her breathing is uncontrollable as he climax. Eddie fully aroused lets out a big sigh, "Damn!"

Sheila turns toward Eddie. She rubs the cheek of Eddie staring into his eyes, "I love you Eddie." They lay there in silence for a moment. Sheila curls up under Eddie. He looks over his shoulder at his cell phone that has been vibrating for the entire time they made love.

Sheila on cloud nine responds to the look Eddie's giving her, "What?"

Eddie Sr. speaks bitterly, "You know what?"

Sheila taken by surprise slides from under Eddie and sits up in the bed. "No, I don't know what. Tell me." She responded.

Eddie turns toward Sheila, "You think I don't know why you're sniffing on me?"

Sheila smirks, "Regardless, it was good. I just wanted to make sure you were clean before I start licking and sucking on you."

Eddie angry, "Don't be sniffing all on me like some lost dog."

Sheila giggles, "OH MY GOD! This not about me this about who's calling you or texting you."

Eddie Sr. not amused pulls the sheets over him ignoring her comment.

Sheila lies in the opposite direction with a big grin on her face. She was thinking to herself that Eddie was the lick'em below Champion in her book and could do no wrong on this night.

The next day Eddie Sr. is up early answering his emails. A few of his gambling buddies sent text messages.

IT'S GOING DOWN AT MY CRIB AT HIGH NOON, Joe had text.

The second text was from Tonya, SORRY ABOUT THE WAY I BEHAVED YESTEDAY. CALL ME!

Third text from Big Mike reads, THOSE BONES CLICKING TODAY AT HIGH NOON. GET DOWN OR LAY DOWN.

Eddie Sr. quickly texts Joe, COUNT ME IN.

Sheila rolls over and looks at Eddie Sr., "Why you all bright-eyed and bushy tailed?"

Eddie looks at Sheila and smirks, "Stop repeating what your great grandma used to say. 'Bright-eyed.' Tis!"

Sheila smiles thinking about last night, "Okay. You're the big Dawg! Where are you going? You haven't spent one weekend at home since we moved here?"

Eddie's speechless for a moment, "Big Dawg!" He barks like a dog playing around. The bedroom door swings open quickly. Victor runs in excited. "Mom, I heard a dog. Where is it?"

Sheila looks over at Eddie Sr., "There it is. That was your dad acting silly."

Victor grabs his dad's pants leg, "Dad, can we have a dog?"

Eddie continues to get dress.

"Vic, you really don't want to have that responsibility of cleaning up somebody else shit." Eddie declares as Sheila stares at him.

"Yes, I do Dad. I'll clean up shit! PLEASE!" Victor stated.

Eddie frowns looking down at Victor, "You better watch your mouth."

"Come here baby." Sheila laughing reaches out to hug Victor.

"Well, he just responded the way you said it. Just maybe you can have a dog. What kind would you like?" She said looking at Eddie Sr.

Victor screams with joy, "YESSS. A pit-bull Mama."

Sheila grabs Victor looks him directly in his eyes, "Wow! Son, those are some very dangerous dogs. I think we should start off with something small first. Okay?"

"Okay Mommy." Victor replies as he hugs her tightly.

Eddie chuckles and mumbles, "I hear all the small innuendos you keep making about dogs. Here is one for you, 'It's a small thing to a giant something small like you use to be,' huh?" He turns and exits the room head out the front door. Sheila confused jumps up dropping the blanket. She is naked and in high pursuit on his heels. She stops at the top of the stairs.

"What was that you said?"

Eddie Sr. grabs the doorknob pausing looking back up the stairs at Sheila.

"You heard me. Put some clothes on. These boys getting too big to see you walking around here naked." He smirks, "Besides it's not sexy."

Sheila offended and angry screams, "FUCK YOU TOO WITH YOUR FAT ASS!"

Eddie Sr. opens the door and walks out, but not before Sheila snaps.

"THAT'S RIGHT … GO AHEAD WALK OUT AND GO TO THAT OTHER BITCH!"

Victor starts to cry.

"HUSH UP LITTLE BOY!"

Eddie Sr. opens the door, looks back up at Sheila and shaking his head turns slams the door. He continues on his journey. Eddie walks into the garage. He moves a few things around and grabs ten grand from underneath some old tires. He stuffs the cash in his pockets jumping into his Range Rover. As the truck warms up, Eddie calls Joe on his car phone.

Joe in the bed with two women leans over one of the girls reaching for the phone. The woman is sleeping and Joe wakes her accidentally. She gets upset with Joe. Joe politely checks her, "You don't have to be here. Now pass me the phone." She reaches for the phone Joe admires Carmen's nice round ass. He smacks her butt while she reaches for the phone. "Thanks Bae!"

"You welcome."

"What's good?" Joe asked

"Damn, kid I thought you weren't going to answer the phone," Eddie said.

"Your boy sitting over here with a double bubble. Shit, I almost didn't answer. What's good?" Joe replied.

"The dice rolling at high noon," Eddie responded.

"Bet that. You heard anything from them people who came by the job?" Joe asked.

Eddie with a slight chuckle, "Hell naw, shit I haven't heard from them sons of bitches."

Carmen slides from under the covers, "It's hot in here." She reveals her breast and navel ring. Joe just watches her as he continues to talk with Eddie.

"Yeah Big Dawg, I hear you on that. Let's just see how it plays out."

Eddie pulling out of the driveway, "Who is that talking in the background?"

"Carmen!"

"Brah, Carmen is one little fine mother-fucker with that fat round ass."

"No doubt about it. I'm looking at it right now. I got Deanna up in here too."

Eddie just shakes his head while driving, "Dude why did I get married? I ask myself that shit all the time."

"It was the right thing to do. You still have your high school sweetheart," Joe replied.

Eddie sarcastically answers, "Yeah okay! On that note I'm gone."

Joe laughs, "Yeah, let me get these girls their morning protein then we can go to breakfast. If you know what I mean?"

"Yes Sir! I'll catch up with you later. I'm at the job," Eddie responded with a hint of frustration.

Eddie steps out of the truck walking into his office building. Looking at Tonya's car parked in the back of the building. Eddie sticks his key in the door and out of nowhere Tonya grabs him around the waist startling him.

"What the Fuck!"

"Hey Eddo!"

Eddie upset quickly opens the door stepping inside pulling Tonya inside. He quickly turns off the alarm. Tonya smelling and looking good pushes up on Eddie as he enters his office.

"Stop touching me it's not right," Eddie said.

Tonya slowly unzips her full length coat revealing her lace bodystocking with miss crouch. Eddie gets an instant erection as Tonya grabs his penis. Tonya pushes Eddie against the desk.

Tonya whispered in the sexiest voice, "I'm sorry about the other day. Let me make it up to you. I know how you like to touch the back of my throat. And I love the way it feels inside my mouth."

She attempts to unzip Eddie's pants. He stops her grabbing her hand. She reverses the hand hold placing Eddie's hand on her nice firm soft breast. Eddie trying to fight off the temptation but Tonya will not have it. He grabs her breast with both hands and Tonya quickly drops his pants and boxers around his ankles.

"No … no … Tonya. Mrs. Best will be walking in any minute," Eddie exclaimed.

Tonya takes Eddie deep into her throat. He falls back placing all his weight on the desk. The alarm chirps as Mrs. Best enters the building. Mrs. Best walks over to her desk to set up when she thought she heard moaning. She stands and walks around toward the office doors. She places her ear on Eddie's office door. She doesn't hear anything and she starts to walk away when the door quickly opens. Tonya abruptly walks out with Eddie on her heels.

"I'm going to see what I can do for you on that deal," Eddie spoke.

Tonya upset doesn't say a word brushing pass Mrs. Best.

"Good Morning!" Mrs. Best said.

Tonya continued on her way out the door without saying a word.

"Good morning Mrs. Best," Eddie responded.

Mrs. Best gives Eddie that shameful nod, "Good morning Mr. Fox."

Weeks later Sheila is shopping after school. She runs into Bryant her brother Reggie's buddy at the checkout counter. Bryant is rocking the latest hip hop fashion with some Air Force One's. He has a fresh shave and his hair twisted nicely. Sheila smiles as Bryant approaches her.

"Look at you. I didn't think you had it in you," Sheila said.

Bryant feeling his own swag smiles looking at Sheila's jeans, "I'm trying to see what that do?"

Sheila burst out laughing, "Boy please. You're crazy. See what, what do?"

Bryant looks at Sheila's butt, "Yeah that."

Sheila places her groceries on the counter, "Just like that, huh? No wine, no dine, just get behind, huh?"

"No it's a little more to it than that," Bryant replied grinning.

Sheila pays for her groceries and pushes her cart to the car with Bryant right beside her.

"And what did my brother Reggie say to you about flirting with me?"

Bryant looks around, "I don't see him here, so why worry about that."

Sheila pushes the remote key to the truck opening the hatch to load the bags.

Bryant assists her placing the bags in the back of the truck. Sheila closes the hatch with the remote. She swings her hair back in Bryant's face, "Well, Bryant thanks for your help."

Bryant steps a little closer to Sheila as she is about to step into the truck.

"It was no problem. But I do have one request." Bryant states.

Sheila sitting inside the truck, "And what might that be?"

Bryant very smooth, "If you ever need someone to talk to other than family, all I ask is that you give me a call." He passes her a piece of paper with his number on it.

"Yeah right! We'll see about that. Bye Bryant."

Sheila closes the car door. Bryant stands at the window. Sheila lets the window down.

"What Bryant? Don't make me be rude and drive off on your ass."

"Those jeans are talking to me."

"What are they saying Bryant? I almost don't want to know."

"Touch me!" He reaches inside the car and touches Sheila's thigh.

Sheila laughs shaking her head in disagreement, "BOY Bye." She backs up out of her parking space.

Moments later, Sheila pulls up in the driveway at home. She begins to take the groceries in the house. Eddie Sr. and Sheila have been getting along for the most part. She notices that the boys have not come out to help her with the bags. She walks to the back room where the boys are. She opens the door and Eddie Sr. is back there with the boys and a puppy.

"Mom, look Dad brought us a dog," Victor said.

E.J. excited, "Yeah Mom this is our dog."

Roosevelt sitting next to Eddie Sr. Eddie Sr. is attempting to train the dog.

"Sit Rocky, sit," Eddie Sr. commands.

Rocky barks and runs around. The boys all laugh because Rocky just runs and barks. He doesn't listen.

Sheila gazes on with sheer delight watching the kids with their dad.

"I don't know why you over there laughing. I'd sure like to see you do better," Eddie Sr. said.

Sheila steps inside the room. "Rocky is his name?"

"Yes," E.J. replied.

"Come here Rocky … come here boy," Sheila called out.

Rocky makes his way over to Sheila tail wagging. She pets him on top of the head.

"Now sit Rocky," Sheila asked.

Rocky sits right next to Sheila. The boys burst out in laughter.

"Oh boy! Mommy how did you do that? Roosevelt asked."

Victor runs over and hugs Rocky around the neck.

"YOU'RE choking him Vic not so tight," Sheila said.

Eddie Sr. looks up at Sheila with a look of regret, "I guess your mom has a way of handling dogs."

Sheila with a lustful eye stares at Eddie Sr. because they hadn't made love since the argument,

"Just call me the dog catcher. Big Dawg, dinner will be ready soon. Are you staying for dessert?"

"I sure will, Mrs. Fox, I'm all in now," Eddie Sr. replied. He smirks looking at those jeans hugging Sheila's curves that appeared to be painted on. Sheila walks over to Eddie Sr. leaning down to give him a kiss, "Thanks."

"What for?" Eddie Sr. asked.

"Making the boys day, and spending time with them," Sheila responded with a big smile.

Eddie reaches his arms up around Sheila's waist pulling her close to him. She bends over giving him a passionate kiss.

E.J. looks on, "Ugh."

Roosevelt covers his eyes not wanting to watch them kiss. Victor continues to rough up Rocky. Rocky runs from Victor. Everyone starts to laugh as Victor repeatedly tries to pick Rocky up. Rocky just kept on barking trying to scare Victor away.

* * *

One afternoon at Sheila's parents' house, Grandma Jean is cooking lunch for her husband James. Tonya walks in the house takes a seat in the kitchen, "Grandma."

"Hey Tonya! You look nice today."

"I guess," Tonya answered nonchalantly.

Tonya was wearing a peanut-butter leather jacket with matching boots and belt by Prada®.

Grandma Jean turns from the stove in Tonya's direction, "Baby, you want something to eat?"

Tonya slumped down in the chair with elbows in her lap and hands under her chin. Grandma stares at Tonya for a second, "Baby did you hear me? I asked if you wanted something to eat."

"No thanks Grandma."

Grandma Jean turns the eye down on the stove and walks over to the table taking a seat in front of Tonya. Grandma Jean concern, "Tonya what's wrong?"

Instantly tears start to stream down Tonya's face. Grandma Jean moves closer to Tonya trying to console her.

"Baby, I can't help you if you don't tell me what's wrong?"

Tonya crying intensifies as she drops her head to the table. Grandma Jean starts to worry as she reaches over pulling Tonya off the table on to her chest, "Shhh! It's going to be okay."

She was trying her best to console Tonya. However, Tonya just cried and held on to her.

Grandpa James is in the backroom watching T.V. with the door open waiting for his lunch.

"JEAN! Where's my lunch woman?" Grandpa James yelled.

"It's just about done," Grandma Jean responded.

"Hell! It's taking long enough. What you had to do? Pluck the chicken," He laughs to himself.

Grandma Jean shakes her head, "Tonya your Grandpa is crazy. You know that right?" She tries to cheer Tonya up.

Tonya laughs through her tears, "That's not funny Grandma."

Grandma Jean lifts Tonya up off her chest wiping her face. "Now tell me what all this crying is about?" Grandma asked.

Tonya mumbles real low, "I'm pregnant," Tonya places her hands on her face in disappointment as the tears stream down her face again.

"That's not so bad Tonya. You have two degrees and you are working on your Masters. You and the baby will be just fine," Grandma Jean said.

Grandma Jean walks over to the stove to check on the food. She stirs the pot with one hand while resting the other hand on her hip in deep thought. She walks back over to Tonya.

Tonya's eyes are bloodshot red from all the crying. She starts to cry again and blurts out, "By a married man Grandma, a married man."

Grandma Jean spoke with great disappointment. "TONYA! How could you allow something like this to happen with all this protection out here nowadays? Tee, you know I don't approve of this. By a married man? What about his wife and her feelings. Tonya!"

Tonya drops her head speaking through her tears, "I know. I didn't mean for it to happen."

"No you didn't. But the fact remains it did happen. Now what Tonya?" Grandma Jean asked with disappointment.

Shanae walks in the house. "Grandma, I want some. I smell that chicken all outside."

She walks into the kitchen to find Tonya crying and goes from zero to ten in seconds, "WHAT'S WRONG TEE?" Shanae asked.

"She'll be okay. Just give her a minute. How are you Shae?" Grandma Jean stated.

"I'm good. What's up with my sister tho?"

Tonya lifts her head to speak but can't get the words out. Shanae gets more upset as she removes her jacket.

"Tell me Tee who did it? We can get it crackin'." Shanae stated.

"Sit your ass down. Nobody's cracking nothing. Wash your hands so you can eat." Grandma said.

Grandpa James frustrated, "Dammit Jean! Get your ass up before I come in there and fix my own plate. That girl knows better than to be messing with a married man."

Shanae surprised, "Oh snap! Is that true Tee?"

Tonya mumbles under her breathe, "Grandpa talks too much." Thinks to herself, *how did he hear us over that T.V. blasting*?

Grandpa James, "I heard that Tonya."

Tonya looks up at Shanae and Grandma Jean dumbfounded shaking her head.

Grandma Jean shakes her head disgusted. "He has lost his mind." She is fixing his sandwich. Grandpa James blurts out, "Yeah! Put mustard on there too."

Shanae looks at her Grandma Jean and whispers, "How does he know you're fixing his sandwich?"

"I don't know. Sometime I think he got cameras in this house." Grandma Jean said.

She walks his plate to the room and James is sleeping. She turns to walk out of the room and James jumps up, "Bring that plate woman. You know I'm joking around Love Bug."

Tonya and Shanae just look at one another without saying a word about how well their grandparents knew one another. Grandma Jean comes back and sits a plate in front of Tonya, "Now eat up, you know you're feeding two now."

Shanae eases away in deep thought about what Grandma Jean and Grandpa James have said. Shanae walks into the next room thinking about what she had just heard. Shanae speaks out to herself, *Pregnant, by a married man. WOW!*"

*   *   *

One month later. Eddie Sr. returns home from one of his late outings. He comes in the house escorted by three men wearing black hoodies. One of the men immediately rushes into the kitchen grabbing Sheila. The gunmen all have their weapons out as they move the family to the living-room. They have the entire family sitting on the couch with the exception of

Eddie Sr. Blue the larger guy out of the hooded men approaches Eddie Sr. sitting on the loveseat.

"I'm going to give you a chance to give me the money without anyone getting hurt. So where is the money," Blue asked.

Eddie Sr. frighten as he looks around at the gunmen, "What money?"

Red, the second in command pulls a roll of duct tape out of his backpack. "So you think it's a game?" Red asked before he started to duct tape the kids' hands and feet. Sheila and Eddie watch helplessly. Red tapes everyone's mouth, but Eddie Sr.

"Where's the money? This is about to get real up in here. Where is it? It's all up to you," Blue said.

Eddie Sr. drops his head pleading, "I don't know what money you're talking about."

Blue very calm, "Okay, have it your way. Red taped Eddie's mouth and hands. Whitey bring that Bitch over here to me."

Sheila panics as Whitey pulls her off the couch. He takes her over to Blue and makes Sheila kneel down in front of Blue. Blue growing inpatient cracks his neck.

"Now tell me where the money is or do I have to hurt your wife?" Blue asked.

Sheila with fear written all over her face tries to stay strong as the boys watch her. Eddie remains silent. Rocky is locked in the basement and is barking up a storm. "That fucking barking is getting on my nerves. Red find that bitch something to eat. If she don't stop barking put that bitch down." Whitey quickly springs into action. Blue reaches down snatches Sheila by her shirt exposing her bra. Sheila's eyes shows fear as she screams from under the duct tape. Tears start to roll down her cheeks. E.J. starts breathing heavily as tears run down his face watching Blue take advantage of his mother. Victor is already crying unable to move he just sobs. Roosevelt just sits quietly with his eyes closed tightly trying to block it all out. Eddie Sr. glances at his family's faces and the sheer look of terror in their eyes almost breaks him. Blue snatches Sheila's hair yanking her head back placing the gun on her breast. Eddie Sr. jumps up to charge Blue. Whitey stops Eddie Sr. in his tracks aiming the gun straight at Eddie's head. Whitey smacks Eddie Sr. with the butt of the gun sending Eddie Sr. back down to the loveseat.

"Time is out for being nice," Whitey said.

Blue pissed off, "Now sit your *wanna* be tough ass down or your family can watch you die."

Blue pushes Sheila to the floor and walks over to Eddie Sr.

"Now you know we mean business. For the last time, where's the fucking money?" Blue asked.

Eddie replies dropping his head trying to figure things all out, "The money isn't here? Now pick my wife up please I'm begging you."

Sheila laying on the floor in shock has lost all sense of reality.

Blue walks and stands over Sheila aiming his gun at her, "Then where's the fucking money if it's not here?"

"Up north, up north…" Eddie Sr. cries out.

Eddie Sr. pleads, "I can pay you more than whoever sent you … please don't hurt my family."

"Oh, and you will pay more or we'll start killing your family." Blue said with a smirk and calm demeanor which struck more fear in Eddie Sr. Red returns from the basement. "All that bitch needed was some love looking at Sheila but talking about Rocky."

"Cool," Blue responded.

Blue lowers his weapon and pulls out his cell-phone calling Pinky the driver.

"Hello!"

Blue speaks with frustration, "Bring the truck around."

Pinky pulls the truck around in front of the house. Blue rushes Eddie Sr. out to the vehicle holding his pistol in his hoodie pocket.

"Eddie, get your punk ass up if you know what's good for you and your family that money better be up north."

Blue leads Eddie to the door, "Here's your chance to save your family. Let's go Red, you and Whitey chill until we get back. Once I get the money, I'll give you a call. If this chump knows what's good for him, he'll give up that cash!"

Blue and Eddie Sr. walk over to a black SUV with tinted windows. The side door opens quickly with a soft female voice, "Where we off too?"

"The Northside." Blue replied.

Pinky drives for about fifteen minutes heading to the north side driving down Lake Shore Drive, it's a chilly night but the city skyline is beautiful "Damn Chicago is beautiful. But the cost of living is too fucking high. So we do what we gotta just to get by. Just to get by … just to get by…."

Blue chuckles, "Pink that's one of your songs."

"Naw!" She merges over into the right lane. "Where am I getting off?" Pinky asked.

Blue looks at Eddie Sr. with pistol in hand, "The lady talking to you playboy. Where we off to?"

"Umm … Irving Park," Eddie responded.

Blue leans forward speaking in Eddie's ear, "This had better be the right spot or an example will be made."

Pinky merges off the expressway exiting on Irving Park Road. Eddie instructs her, "Turn right on Broadway than a left on Gordon. I'm not sure who told you about this money but it's not mines. The person this money belongs to is not going to appreciate you hitting his stash house. He will kill all of us."

Blue gives a slight chuckle, "Man, you really think I give a fuck. Who you talking about? Big Randy! MOTHER FUCK BIG RANDY, he ain't no fucking body to us."

Eddie astonish that Blue knows who the money belongs to and tries to catch on to Blue's voice.

Back at the Fox residence Red and Whitey have taped the boys' feet together and carried Sheila off to the bedroom. Sheila lies on the bed. Red starts to undress her with the bedroom door open. Sheila's breasts are exposed bouncing around and the kids watching. Sheila tries to fight them off but they over power her. Red cuts the tape off her legs removing her pants and underwear. The kids could see what was about to happen. E.J. leans forward blocking Roosevelt and Victor's view as tears stream down their faces. Red unzips his pants exposing himself. Sheila squirms around not giving in until Red places the pistol in her face. Red then forces himself on Sheila.

Whitey aroused, "Damn Gee she got some nice firm boobs for a bitch with three kids." He touches one pinching her nipple.

Sheila lies lifeless as tears stream down her face. She could only feel shame as Eddie Jr. looked on. Red puts on a condom forces Sheila's legs apart, "Yeah, a pretty bitch like this thinks she too much for guys like us Whitey."

"Not no more. She just another pretty bitch out here," Whitey said laughing.

Red takes complete advantage of Sheila thrusting hard and deep inside of her as he could. Whitey looks outside of the room to the boys on the couch turns to leave the room.

"Where you going Dawg! Don't you want this bitch."

"Nigga hell naw. It's first or nothing with me." Whitey laughs, "With your thirsty ass."

Red trying to rip Sheila's insides out thrusting hard as he could in and out of Sheila, "You never had a fine bitch like this one," Red said.

Sheila's eyes are tightly closed as tears continue streaming down her cheeks. Sheila wanting it to be over just stops fighting hoping it would end quickly.

Whitey nods his head walks out the room closing the door behind him so the kids couldn't see anymore. Moments later Red walks out the room while Sheila lays on the bed in shock. Tears fall down E.J.'s face as he screams from under the duct tape, "MOM … MOM…."

Whitey gets up out of the chair jokingly, "Man Dawg, you making love or what?"

Red slightly exhausted, "Fuck you! She got that bomb pussy."

Whitey laughs, "Man you stupid that's not your bitch."

Red replies, "She's ready for you."

Whitey insulted, "Fool, I told you I don't do sloppy seconds."

"Yeah, okay. I might do seconds if they don't hurry the hell up," Red responded.

Whitey gives Red a hard look nodding his head in disapproval, "Man you're fucked up in the head. You know that right?"

Red laughs, "Fuck what you talking about? Whatever!"

Whitey just shakes his head in disbelief and laughs, "You a fool with it. What the fuck is taking Blue so fucking long? Something must have gone wrong."

Back over at the safe house Blue has Eddie walk inside first. The basement apartment is fully furnished. Pinky comes in behind Blue. "Shit, this one nice apartment I could live here," Pinky said.

"Yeah, it is. But let's get this money. Kneel down motherfucker," Blue said.

Eddie kneels down in the living room.

"Pinky tapes his feet and hands together before I get this money," Blue said.

Pinky a small woman quickly tapes Eddie's hands and feet together. Eddie is a large guy she struggles getting both hands together.

Eddie pleads for his life. "I'm going to tell you where the money is. I wouldn't have brought you here if I wasn't. Just take the money and go PLEASE! PLEASE.... The money is in the back room in the closet."

Blue instantly runs to the back room closet.

Pinky stands over Eddie Sr. with a pistol pointed at him. "I kind of admired you, but you're a lame ass chump just like the rest of the chumps we dumped out their pockets. You're up in here begging for your life. I thought you were a boss. Tis … what a waste. I said you would be different."

Eddie's entire life flashes before his eyes while lying down on the floor. He thinks back to high school when they had pulled a prank on his friend Joe. Joe was so upset that he had gone to Eddie mom's house and told. Eddie kind of grinned about that thought. Mrs. Anne Fox, Eddie's mom has always been supportive of Eddie; however, Mr. Steve Fox was really tough on Eddie. Eddie's mind drifts off to when Sheila was in the hospital having E.J. He's sitting in the hospital room chair holding E.J. up so his family and friends could see E.J. through the window.

Blue runs back in the living room with a gym bag. "I got it." Eddie snaps out of his daydream back into a nightmare to the sound of Blue's voice. "There's another bag back there."

"WHERE?" Pinky asked.

"In the back closet. Go grab it."

Pinky takes off for the back room not knowing that Blue was on her trail. She reaches in the closet to look for the other bag. She doesn't see one. She comes out the closet to find Blue standing there with the pistol pointed at her. "What the fuck you on Blue?"

Blue doesn't say a word. He just stares at her.

Pinky stares Blue down, "What? Whatever you going to do, do it."

Blue cracks up laughing. "The money is hanging there in the bag."

Pinky unsure if Blue is going to shoot her in the back just turns to grab it. Pinky thinks to herself *I know this mother fucker is not to be trusted*? She pulls the bag down off the hook and turns back around and Blue is gone. She quickly moves to the living room. Blue is talking with Red.

"We got the money," Blue said.

Red smiles, "We about to smoke one."

"Naw Red. Go ahead and wrap it up. Make sure no one can get away," Blue said.

"Yep!"

You hear Red telling Whitey in the background just before the phone call ends, "We good. Blue said we can wrap it up and get up out of here. Make sure nobody can get loose."

Whitey excited, "That's what's up."

"We on that Blue," Red stated.

The phone call ends.

"What about this bitch? She's laying here lifeless." Whitey asked.

Red smirks, "Leave her right there. I might double back for some more of that thang." Red winks his eye at Sheila hoping to get a response. Sheila just lies there completely naked and uncovered. Red quickly grabs the duct tape pulling Sheila's legs together wrapping the tape around them. Red is making sure the boys tape is tight and they cannot get loose.

"I'm ready to bounce," Whitey said.

"Yes Sir. We out the back door," Red stated.

Pinky and Blue are standing over Eddie.

"Pinky tape his mouth," Blue demanded.

Pinky a little hesitant about turning her back to Blue steps around to the other side so she could watch Blue.

Blue with a slight chuckle gives Pinky a nasty look, "Now if I was going to slump your ass I would have done so when you were in the closet."

"So you were thinking about it?"

"No, not until you looked at me like I was about to. Then it crossed my mind. Grab the bag and wait for me in the truck."

Pinky grabs the small bag off the floor and heads out the door. Eddie sits quietly thinking about his high school love Sheila. Blue picks up the big bag toss it up on his shoulder and looks at Eddie. Eddie thinks of his parents and how they had raised him in church to be a good man. A vision of Anne Fox and Steve Fox appears in Eddie's mind the next thing he heard was

Blue speaking about what took place in the room with Pinky, "No Bitch can be trusted not even yours!" BANG! Blue walks out the door to the SUV. Pinky slightly paranoid when Blue got inside the truck.

"What the fuck was that?" Pinky asked.

"Nothing, I just put one in his leg. He'll live."

Pinky pulls off slowly to avoid any suspicion.

* * *

At METRO PRISON day-room it's noon and the prisoners have gathered around to watch the news as they always do at noon.

BREAKING NEWS; "Hi, I'm Michelle Matthews reporting live from Broadway and Gordon on this cold winter like day. What was discovered today seems like the making of a mob movie. As you can see behind me the police have blocked off this two level condo building. One man was found inside left for dead with a gunshot to the back of the head execution style. The neighbors thought they heard a gunshot and reported it to the authorities. When the police arrived on the scene they found known real estate broker Eddie Fox Sr. an owner of the complex critically shot in the back of the head. This is Michelle Matthews reporting live from KREW T.V. back to you in the studio."

"Hi, I'm Eugene reporting from KREW T.V. What a horrible story to start off this cold wintery day.

"I have been instructed that we have more breaking news. Okay, Brett take us away."

"Hi this is Brett Anthony reporting live from the block of slain victim Eddie Fox Sr. The police have stopped all traffic down this street. Insiders say that the family of Eddie Fox Sr. was found duct taped in this middle class neighborhood. They also stated his wife had been raped and duct taped as well. This story is starting to take the form of an episode of the Black Sopranos. This is Brett Anthony reporting Live from the scene. Back to Eugene in the studio."

Eugene positioning his chair for the camera, "We'll return after a word from our sponsors."

Big Randy jumps up out of his seat running to the phone. The phone rings.

Automated phone system replies, "This call is from RANDY! Press five to accept the call or press seven to decline. If you wish to block all future calls, dial nine now."

Joe presses five on the other end of the phone, "What's up B.R.?"

Randy frantic, "I don't know. Tell me what's going on?"

Joe really nervous about the situation, "All I know is what was said on the news."

Randy angry, "Whoever, pulled this stunt just made a big mistake. Find out who it was and trust it will be dealt with."

Joe thinking to himself that it was Big Randy who sent somebody to Eddie Sr.'s house the last time.

Big Randy yells, "JOE! You hear me?"

"Yeah, I got my ear to the ground," Joe responded.

"Make sure you keep me posted," Big Randy said.

"I'm on my way out to the hospital now," Joe replied.

Big Randy takes a look around the phone room sucking his teeth as if someone inside had something to do with it. "I'm going to call you back tomorrow at the same time. Have some news for me."

"Yep, later!" Joe ends the call.

Joe at home walks to his den removing a 9mm handgun from his desk. He places the pistol in the small of his back. He walks over grabs his jacket looking at himself in a full-length mirror by the door. He speaks to the mirror. Eye's bloodshot red from crying, "Trust none, and suspect all. Somebody is going to pay for this." He heads out the door.

After a long day at the police station the kids go to Sheila's parents' home. Roosevelt and Victor are sleeping in Shanae's room. E.J. is in the room with Grandpa James watching television. The phone rings. Grandma Jean answers.

"Hello!" No one responds. "Hello! They must have the wrong number." She hangs the phone up.

Shanae is at the hospital with her Aunt Sheila. The police are in the room questioning her about what happened. Sheila lies in the bed unresponsive to their line of questioning. Officer Glen seemed unfazed by the torture that Sheila had just been through,

"Okay when he had sex with you. Was he fully dressed or did he get naked?"

Shanae furious, "SHE WAS RAPED DAMMIT!"

"I'm only asking to see if he had any distinguishing marks on his body that she could recall. Like a tattoo or cut."

"NO! You made it sound like it was consensual." Shanae replied as tears started to flow down her cheeks. Sheila upset tries to sit up in the bed getting light headed. She falls back quick and hard. Shanae snaps, "Leave her alone now. GET THE FUCK OUT!"

The nurse rushes in when she hears all the commotion, "And what's going on in here Officers?"

"Just routine line of questioning?" Officer Glen responded.

"I'm afraid I'm going to have to ask you officers to leave until this young lady is feeling better." Nurse Nina walks over and passes tissue to Shanae to wipe her face as she checks Sheila's pulse.

"Will be back so get your story together?" Officer Glen said.

"SEE, THAT'S WHAT THE FUCK I'M TALKING ABOUT. What story?" Shanae responded giving Officer Glen an angry look.

Officer Martin nods in his disapproval, "Ma'am. We'll check back with you later."

The Officers turn and exit the room. Sheila looks up at Nurse Nina with a daze look. "Am I free to go home?" Sheila asked.

The nurse smiles, "Yes, you can go home as soon as you feel better. You're not in jail. All you need to do is get better and sign yourself out."

Sheila in a really weak voice, "Where are the papers? I need to go see my husband."

Shanae holding in all her emotions thinking Eddie Sr. had died.

Nurse Nina takes Sheila's temperature and speaks very pleasantly,

"I'll check on your papers. All of your tests have come back negative for any STDs and we're checking for DNA. I'll go get your paperwork started." Nurse Nina walks out with her chart. Shanae grabs her gym bag pulling out underclothes and a designer sweat suit. She helps Sheila slide into her underwear and fasten her bra.

Sheila is moving gingerly. Shanae grabs a brush out of the bag brushes Sheila's hair into a ponytail. Shanae tries to make small talk, "Auntie Sheila, your hair has really grown."

Nurse Nina returns to the room with Dr. Greyhouse. He's carrying her chart and papers. Dr. Greyhouse passes his chart to Nurse Nina removes his light from his top pocket looking into Sheila's eyes.

"Look left young lady. Look right."

Sheila does as the doctor instructed.

"Note that her vitals are good. If she feels that she's ready to be released then we should. The nurse will go over your prescriptions; however, we are releasing you under your wishes at your own risk, not the hospital's recommendation. I think you need to stay for more observation." Dr. Greyhouse said before he walked out.

"You are good to go Mrs. Fox. I need you to sign here and here."

Sheila reaches for the clipboard.

"Your prescriptions should be ready. Stop at the pharmacy on the first level to pick it up. The crème that you're receiving will help with the vaginal swelling. You may experience some soreness from the force penetration. If you have any problems bleeding or other problems do not hesitate to return to the emergency room. Do you understand?" Nurse Nina asked.

Sheila nods her head in agreement.

"That's not good enough Mrs. Fox. I'm going to need you to speak before I can release you."

"Yes, Nurse. I understand," Sheila responded. Sheila slides off the bed with Shanae assisting her, "Nae-nae is this really happening?"

"Yes Auntie!" She helped Sheila put on her jacket.

"Here slide your arm in here Auntie," Shanae said softly.

"Oh! I feel like I been in a train wreck," Sheila exclaimed.

Nurse Nina opens the door for Sheila and Shanae exit. Sheila walks gingerly along Shanae. They picked up the prescription then drove to the north side of the city to check on Eddie Sr.'s well-being.

The Chicago Police Department quickly assigned a detective to the case. Eddie's parents were well known in the community for good services provided by the church. Eddie Sr. had long strayed away from the church life. Detective Strong stops by the Fox's home to inform them of the situation. Detective strong pulls in front of the Fox home driving an unmarked car. He quickly proceeds to the door. He knocks and rings the bell.

Mr. Fox answers the door. "Yes officer?"

"How are you Sir? Are you the parent of Eddie Fox?"

Panic strikes Mr. Fox's face, "Yes, what is this about?"

"Sir your son has been shot," Detective Strong stated.

Mr. Fox's heart sinks in his chest. He drops his head thinking, "Oh Lord, what have this boy done."

"He's in critical condition. I think you and the family should get over to the hospital as soon as possible." Officer Strong hands Mr. Fox the address on the report.

"Thanks Officer, Strong that is?" Mr. Fox asked.

"Yes Sir." Here's my card if you have any questions.

Mr. Fox closes the door slowly and watches Officer Strong pull away. Mr. Fox goes into the family room where the family was preparing to go downtown for lunch. Anne Fox sense that something was wrong the way Mr. Fox entered the room in silence.

Mrs. Fox calls out to her husband by his pet name as he stands in a daze. "FOXY!"

He leans against the wall trying to gather his thoughts. He thinks how he worked so hard to keep his children out of harm's way. He lives in a middle class community with a low crime rate and a good school system. He mumbles out, "What's the point?"

Mrs. Fox quickly runs to his aid, "Foxy what's happening."

"We all need to get to the hospital. Eddie has gotten shot."

"Let's go, now!" Mrs. Fox exclaimed.

Everyone rushes on their coats and exit out the house quickly. Mr. Fox pulls out his late model S class Mercedes. On the drive to the hospital Mrs. Fox holds her husband's hand in silent prayer.

Eddie Sr. fighting for his life is undergoing an emergency surgery. Eddie Sr.'s parents are there with his sister Edra and her husband Frank. Everyone sits in silent prayer waiting on the outcome. Sheila and Shanae abruptly walk into the waiting area. Mrs. Anne is the first to see her daughter-in-law. She rushes over to Sheila embracing her as tears start to run down her cheeks. Shanae takes a seat next to Frank and drops her head in disbelief.

"Frank how is my uncle Eddie doing?" Shanae asked.

Edra rocking back and forth responds, "He's in there fighting for his life. All we can do now is pray."

Frank quickly consoles his wife wrapping his arm around her. The tears stream down Edra's face uncontrollably.

Shanae trying to be strong cannot control her emotions anymore, "I'm so sorry this happened. Why can't it be me in there instead? Eddie has helped so many people. He doesn't deserve this. It should have been me," Shanae cried out. Edra turns to console Shanae holding her hands. "This is no fault of yours. Don't take the blame."

"I could of done something. Something!" Shanae cries.

Shanae pulls away headed for the restroom. On her way to the restroom Shanae sees Tonya and Kim quickly approaching.

"SHANAE!" Tonya yells.

Shanae stands still until they're right before her.

"Nae! How is Uncle Eddie doing?" Tonya asked.

Shanae fighting to hold her tears back, "It's not looking good."

Sadness instantly strikes Tonya's face, "Where's Auntie Sheila?"

"She's around the corner with Eddie's family," Shanae replied.

Kim grabs Tonya's hand as they slowly walk around the corner.

Kim whispers to Tonya, "Should we be here? Do you think that they know?"

Tonya cuts her eyes at Kim and squeezes Kim's hand.

Mr. and Mrs. Fox stand to greet Tonya. Tonya speaks in a soft voice.

"Hello!"

Mrs. Fox hugs Tonya tightly, "I didn't know you were with child."

"How far along are you?"

Tonya is reluctant to say, "Four months. How did you know?"

"Your skin is so radiant," Mrs. Fox replied.

"This is my friend Kim from Law school," Tonya said.

Kim smiles and waves at everybody as she sits next to Edra. Mrs. Fox continues chatting with Tonya for a second before Tonya approaches her Aunt Sheila. Sheila has her head down in her palms when Tonya reaches down to embrace her.

"Auntie, how are you doing?" Tonya asked.

Sheila lifts her head and her face is puffy from all the crying she has been doing. Sheila tries to speak through her tears lifting her head up with tears streaming down, "I'm okay. I just want my husband to be okay. LORD PLEASE!" Sheila starts breathing heavily while Edra tries to comfort her sister-in-law rubbing her back. Sheila starts to rock back and forth praying through her tears. Tonya gets emotional instantly tears run down her cheeks. Tonya begins nodding her head no. Kim runs over to Tonya's aid.

"No … no ... no ... this can't be happening," Tonya cried out.

Kim hugs Tonya tightly to comfort her.

"What will my little cousins do without their dad?" Tonya asked.

Kim whispers in Tonya's ear, "What will you do?"

Tonya pulls away from Kim not replying to her statement. Moments later everyone has settled when

Shanae makes her way back from the restroom. It appears as if everyone had their own silent prayer going. Shanae takes a seat next to her Aunt Sheila and joins the silent prayer. One hour passes without any news about the surgery.

Minutes later Dr. T. Jamison approaches the family. Eddie's mom was the first to see the doctor standing there. She jumps up immediately,

"How is he doc?" Momma Fox asked?

The entire family turns in anticipation waiting on Dr. T. Jamison to respond. He takes a deep breath then exhales, "The operation went well."

"Thank you Lord!" Mrs. Fox exclaimed.

"However, the next few days will be the most important. We have induced a coma so that the brain can start to heal. He's still in a very critical position. We'll have to monitor him closely over the next 72 hours," Dr. T. Jamison stated.

Sheila very upset, "Can I please see my husband?"

"Yes, but that is limited to his wife and parents only and one person at a time while he remains in the Trauma Ward. Who wants to go first? Mom or Dad?" Doctor Jamison asked.

Eddie's parents look at one another and Mrs. Fox speaks, "Take his wife in first," Mrs. Fox replied.

Sheila replies very emotionally, "Thanks Momma Fox."

"This way Ma'am." Dr. Jamison escorts Sheila to the Trauma Unit.

Sheila enters the room pausing looking at all the machines that Eddie Sr. was hooked up to. She barely recognized Eddie as she pulled up a chair to sit beside him. She grabs one of Eddie's hands holding on to it. She slowly looks up to see Eddie's eyes taped close.

His head was so swollen that he didn't look anything like himself. She looked at all the monitors and wires hooked up to Eddie. She shakes her head no before dropping her head on the side of Eddie's bed.

Dr. Jamison comes back in to check Eddie's vitals when he notices Sheila has not moved since he left the room earlier.

"Mrs. Fox … Mrs. Fox," Dr. Jamison called out.

Sheila was unresponsive to the calling of her name. Quickly Dr. Jamison rushes over to Sheila lifting her head. Sheila is cold and sweating with her eyes rolled up in the back of her head.

"NURSE! NURSE! Get in here." Dr. Jamison hits the nurse call button. The nurses quickly aid rushing a gurney into the room and placing Sheila on top. They rush Sheila down the hall pass the rest of the family members.

Tonya yells, "WHAT'S WRONG WITH MY AUNTIE?"

"She has gone into shock," Dr. Jamison replied.

Shanae runs to the restroom to call her Grandma Jean.

Tonya quickly pulls out her cell phone calling her Uncle Reggie.

At the Harris' home Roosevelt is still sleeping. Victor's watching television with Grandpa James. E.J. sits outside with Uncle Reggie and a few of his longtime friends. Reggie is furious, about what has taken place with his sister Sheila.

"This is the second time somebody fucked with my sister. Dawg, I'm a deal with it now. I don't give a fuck who it is," Reggie said.

Dave one of the old shot callers from back in the day, "Yeah, this chump then crossed the line. They act like they don't know what we do."

Eric more of a ladies man has been known to take care of business in the streets. "Just when I thought I layed it down these lame niggas pull it," Eric exhales the weed smoke and nods in agreement, "Yeah! This that shit I do like."

Bryant extended his hand for the blunt, "No doubt. These fools out here reckless. They have no clue how dirty we can get."

Lil Rob the quiet type was the go-getter out of the crew. He would just nod yes or no never saying much. It had been rumored that Lil Rob's brother Big Kurt had got picked up for talking about a double murder Lil Rob had done so he just nodded in agreement or disagreement. Lil Rob hits the blunt he exhales and speaks very calmly, "Yep! I want them to feel what we feel."

Everyone pauses and glance at Lil Rob.

Eric laughs nodding his head, "That's what's up!"

Uncle Reggie has always been like the ringleader of the click nods in agreement. "It's going to be some slow singing and flower bringing in Chic-Raq. I don't give a fuck who these clowns plugged with. They can all get it."

"IF MY ALARM STARTS RINGING," E.J. blurts out.

They all laugh.

"My Dad always listens to Biggie," E.J. said. He started to think of Eddie Sr. and tears fill his eyes.

"Oh, they got my Lil Man crying. I'm laying niggas down," Reggie said.

"You think Lil Man should be hearing all this?" Dave asked.

"Yeah, he needs to hear this. Who knows maybe one day he may have to take care of some business out here. Ain't no loyalty out here with these youngsters," Reggie stated.

Grandma Jean pushes the screen door open frantically holding the cordless phone in her hand. "REGGIE!"

Everyone turns toward Mrs. Harris when they hear the sound of panic in her voice.

"Mom what's wrong?" Reggie asked.

"Your sister is having some kind of complications. I need you to take me to the hospital now," Grandma Jean demanded extending her hand for E.J. to come inside as he dropped his head.

She pulls E.J. inside hugging him tightly as tears ran down his face.

E.J. cries his little heart out walking toward Grandma Jean. She starts to tear up watching her Lil Man so upset and thinking about the whole ordeal.

At the hospital Reggie, Bryant, along with Grandma Jean rush inside. They run into Kim and Tonya in the lobby. They all greet one another quickly.

"So where are they?" Grandma Jean asked.

"Uncle Eddie in the Trauma ward and Auntie Sheila in ICU."

Tonya replied. They're about to walk off when Joe comes in the door looking around. Joe recognizes them and immediately walks over.

Kim takes a good look at Joe and whisper to Tonya, "Who is that?"

"That's Eddie's best friend Joe," Tonya said.

"He can be my best friend too," Kim responded.

Tonya gives Kim a hard look, "Really? Bitch right now?"

Joe catches up with everyone as they walk through the hospital.

"Hello Mrs. Harris," Joe said.

"Hello Joseph!" Mrs. Jean Harris replied.

The guys acknowledged one another with a simple head nod.

Joe taps Reggie on the shoulder, "Let me holla at you bro!"

Reggie slows down to talk with Joe. Joe stops walking and Reggie stops as well. Bryant stops a few feet from them as they chat. Grandma Jean, Tonya and Kim continue to Sheila's room.

Reggie and Joe exchange a half hug with a handshake, "What's up Joe?"

Joe with a very angry look on his face grits his teeth, "Man, have you or your guys heard anything about what went down?"

Reggie runs his palm under his chin, "Hell no! Trust and believe I got those hitters out there lurking around. The police are all over the hood so it's tough to move like we do. You feel me?"

"Reggie, I'm going to need you to keep me in play on this one. My Man Eddie didn't deserve this. I'll make it worth your while to keep me in on this one," Joe said.

"Don't even trip, this one on me. But I'll keep you posted," Reggie replied. The elevator door opens and Grandma Jean signals for them to come along. They walk quickly to catch up.

At the Recovery Area Grandma Jean enters Sheila's room everyone else stands at the window. "Hey Sweetheart, how are you doing?"

Sheila very groggy and in pain with wires attached to her and an I.V. "Hey Mom, I'm okay. I really messed up this time. Huh?" A tear falls from Sheila's eye.

"None of this is your fault," Momma Jean replied. She grabs a wash pale fills it with water comes to Sheila's bedside gently cleaning her face. She goes to the window and pulls the curtain. Sheila was very quiet as her mother washes her up. She adjusts Sheila's bed so she could brush her hair.

"How are the boys Mom?"

"They're doing fine. But you know they are worried about you and Eddie. Besides, that dog of yours is giving James a run for his money. I walked in the bedroom and James and Rocky were having a tug-of-war over the newspaper," Grandma Jean chuckles.

Sheila very sad, "Mom, you think the boys would be alright if I wasn't around?"

She pulls Sheila's ponytail tightly, "Huh? Whatever are you talking about? Girl, hush your mouth with that foolishness. Besides you are going to be fine. You have a family that loves you and three boys who need you." She finished combing Sheila's hair walks over to the window pulling the curtain back. Shanae, Tonya, Kim, Reggie, Bryant and two officers from the other hospital Officer Glen and Officer Cole are standing in the window. Sheila's face fills with fear instantly.

"Mom close…." Sheila blacks out and goes into a panic attack. Her body starts to shake and her eye's roll up in the top of her head. She has a very difficult time breathing. Shanae takes off for the nurse's station as Grandma Jean yelled for help and rang the call button.

Three nurses rush in the room. One quickly pulls the curtain close while the other two check on Sheila. They quickly inject Sheila with a shot to calm her down.

"What's going on with my child?" Momma Jean asked.

In a stern voice Nurse Darlene spoke, "I'm going to have to ask you to step out the room momentarily. PLEASE ma'am!"

Grandma Jean quickly exits the room while she is looking back at the Nurses work on Sheila. Shanae meets her Grandma at the door hugging her and crying.

Over in the Trauma Ward the Fox family sits patiently. Everyone appears to be exhausted from all the waiting. Joe has been to the restroom repeatedly trying to get it together before interacting with the Fox Family. Joe steps out of the restroom and Tonya and Kim are headed in his direction back over to the Trauma Ward. The three of them approaches the Fox family at the same time. Instantly Mrs. Fox jumps up to hug Joe. She looked at Joe as her second son, because Eddie and Joe were more like brothers than friends. She hugs Joe tightly and he hugs her just as tight.

"I've been wondering about you?" She kisses Joe on the cheek.

Mr. Fox stands to greet Joe with a firm handshake.

"Thanks for coming Joe," Mr. Fox said.

"It's not a problem. You know Eddie is like my brother."

Edra stands to hug Joe and tears just flow out, "Hey Joe Joe."

"Hey Baby Sis." Joe hugged Edra until she could calm down and stop crying.

"You okay?" Joe asked.

She nods no.

"Where is Frank?" Joe asked.

Edra wiping away the last of her tears, "He went to his parents to pick up the kids."

Joe trying to appear upbeat, "So how's my man doing?"

"We've been waiting forever to hear back from the doctor," Mrs. Fox responded.

Edra is about to sit down when Dr. Harpey walks up. The room goes silent as Dr. Harpey speaks looking over his medical chart.

"Fox family, I have some good news. We have reduced Eddie's coma status. He is breathing on his on."

Mrs. Fox lets out a deep breathe, "Thank you Lord!"

"However, he is still unresponsive," Dr. Harpey stated.

Edra and the family have a look of confusion.

"Dr. Harpey, what exactly does that mean?" Edra asked.

"It means that Eddie is in a vegetative state of mind. He may make a full recovery and he may not. I must tell you only time will tell with the proper medical care. We'll give him the best medical care available, but he is going to have a rough road ahead. I'm sorry," Dr. Harpey said.

Tears start running down Tonya's cheeks. Mrs. Fox breaks down in the middle of the waiting area, "LORD! What have I done to deserve this? Not my baby!"

The tears stream down Tonya's face uncontrollable Kim turns to console her. Mr. Fox holds Edra and his wife. Joe trying to hold it all together for the family is overwhelmed. He quickly walks away from everyone.

Edra yells out, "JOE JOE don't do anything stupid PLEASE! No more no more killing." Edra wipes away her tears and console her mom and dad. Mr. Fox hung on to Edra's last word, "KILLING?"

"Edra do you know something about this? What's going on here?"

"No daddy. We are a blessed family we'll get through this together," Edra said in the most innocent voice.

Outside in front of the hospital Joe is pacing back and forth furious that his boy is fighting for his life. His cell phone rings.

"Hello!" Joe answered.

This call is from a Federal Prison to accept press five.

Instantly Joe presses five fighting back his emotions.

"What's up B.R.?" Joe asked.

"You tell me that's why I'm calling?" Big Randy replied.

Joe unable to control his emotions his voice cracks, "Man! Shit is fucked up. My boy in there in a vegetative state, and I don't know shit about what happened."

Big Randy knows the phone calls are recorded takes the passive approach, "Damn Dawg! I'm sorry that happened to your guy. Don't go get yourself in any trouble. Just relax. You can rest assure that everything will come out. Trust that people love to talk about what they did. Especially when they think that they got away with it," Big Randy stated furiously.

Joe thinks about the recorded calls, "Yup! I'm feeling you on that. We just have to see how this one plays out. Later."

"Oh yeah by the way, a couple of the guys will come get up with you so you can finish that unfinished business. One!" B.R. said.

Joe nods, "Cool, that's what's up." The call ends.

*   *   *

Back over in the Recovery Room Sheila's mom is sitting bedside with her. Sheila continues to moan deeply in her sleep. Mrs. Harris just sits and listens. Sheila is recalling her infidelity in a deep sleep.

Her legs are pent up on her shoulders as this guy strokes her slowly. In the heat of the moment she screams "HARDER OH! OH SHIT!!!"

He digs deeper into her the only image you could see was his back penning her legs back.… Sheila reaches up grabbing both ankles giving this man more room to push deeper inside of her. He grabs the headboard and pounds away on Sheila as her eyes close tightly.

Sweat drips down in Sheila's face as he works that pussy over.

He cries out, "DAMN GIRL!"

"Yes, Baby! Yes … get this pussy baby it's yours!" Sheila exclaims.

Mrs. Harris just watches Sheila squirming and moaning in her sleep.

Sheila calls out, "Yes Bry. Yes … get it baby."

Mrs. Harris grows a little more concern as Sheila calls out another man's name. Sheila begins breathing hard in her sleep. "OH SHIT BRYANT!!! OH OH!! AHHH!!!"

Mrs. Harris doesn't disturb Sheila's dream. Sheila lies there with a big smile on her face. Mrs. Harris tries to put it all together. Sheila's dream continues. Bryant falls to the side of Sheila after they both climax. They both begin to kiss one another passionately. He begins to kiss her breast as she rubs the top of his head. Bryant stops, looking Sheila in her eyes. "You know you're one beautiful woman. So how was it?"

"You have to ask. It was alright. You've done better," She giggles.

"What? I was working that ass over. You know it," Bryant said.

"Yeah! It was really good. As long as you got a face I got a place to sit," Sheila cracks up laughing.

"Oh that's what we on? You crazy, but it's all good with me."

Sheila gets quiet and rolls over on Bryant's chest in deep thought.

Bryant concern, "What are you thinking about Babe?"

"You already know?" Sheila said.

"So what is it you think I know that I don't know?"

Sheila's entire mood changes from happy to sad.

"You know my niece is pregnant by my husband," Sheila said.

Bryant shocked, "WHAT THE FUCK!"

Sheila's medication is wearing off she could hear people talking in her hospital room.

"So Doctor, what's wrong with my daughter?" Mrs. Harris asked.

"Your daughter has endured a great deal of trauma. She's under a great deal of stress with all that has happened in the last 72 hours. These reoccurring episodes your daughter is experiencing are called Anxiety Attacks. I'm going to prescribe something to help her relax. For now I'll give her another injection to calm her. It will also help her sleep," Dr. M. Duke explained. Dr. Duke injects the medication into her I.V. Sheila instantly drifts off into a deep sleep picking up where she left off.

"Yeah, I know that baby is his," Sheila explains to Bryant as they lay next to one another.

"Damn! How that happened? You're sure about this?" Bryant asked.

Sheila speaks sarcastically, "They Fucked! What do you mean? How did that happened?" Her sarcasm turns to sorrow and anger.

"How does that make you feel? If it was me somebody would be getting scraped off the sidewalk. Real talk." Bryant just shakes his head in disbelief. Sheila slides out of the bed naked walking to the bathroom to use it. She sits quietly on the toilet with the door open looking at Bryant as he lies in bed. She wipes herself washes her hands. She strolls back to the bed with the sexiest walk with a look of deceit. She crawls back in the bed like a panther.

"What are you thinking about with that devious look on your face?" Bryant asked.

"I'm thinking that I want to teach his ass a lesson. I gave him three beautiful boys and nine years of my life. And this is how he repays me by getting my niece pregnant?"

"I'm game. What's up?" Bryant said very quickly.

"I'm thinking you could rob his ass," Sheila said.

Bryant laughs, "You're crazy, for what some real-estate?"

Sheila trying to convince him eases down to Bryant's manhood rubbing on him. "If you think real estate paid for all we have you're clearly mistaken."

"Oh really? What do you know that I don't?" Bryant asked curiously.

"I know that Eddie Sr. is holding for some big time dope boy."

"Who?"

"Big Randy?"

"I know you are not talking about Big Randy from out west?"

"I don't know where he is from, but I know Eddie holds for him."

Sheila gives Bryant a seductive look and kisses his manhood, "I know you aren't scared, are you?"

Bryant hesitates, "I fear none, but dude like the mayor around here."

Sheila licks the tip of his manhood, "You wouldn't do it for me?"

Bryant anticipating Sheila taking him deep in her throat, "Yes, I do anything for that. Don't stop."

Sheila teases him a little and stops, "Once it's done you can have all of me you want and whenever you want." She stands in the front of the bed teasing Bryant as she slaps her butt hard looking back at him.

Sheila is tossing and turning in the bed as her Mom watches and listens to her talk in her sleep. Shanae enters the room.

"Grandma, how's Auntie Sheila doing?" Shanae asked.

"She's okay, but she's been tossing and turning since I've been here. I think once she gets some rest she'll be just fine," Grandma Jean responded.

Shanae's reluctant to speak not knowing if Auntie Sheila could hear her. Shanae whispers, "Grandma…"

Grandma Jean kind of irritated by Sheila's dream snaps, "What now Nae-nae?"

"Umm! Uncle Eddie is stable and breathing on his own."

Grandma Jean closes her eyes to give a silent prayer, "Thank God!"

"Yeah, but…." She looks at Sheila to see if she is sleeping.

Grandma Jean replies, "Your Aunt is sleep. Wild animals couldn't wake her."

"But… what child?" Grandma Jean asked.

"He's in a vegetative state," Shanae said.

Grandma Jean's facial expression went from happy to sad real quick.

"Oh no! For God's sake no!" Grandma Jean starts to rock back and forth with her eyes closed. Shanae runs over to her Grandma embraces her rocking back and forward with her. At that moment Sheila screams, "NO…NO…NO. I CHANGED MY MIND NO! PLEASE DON'T!"

Shanae and Grandma Jean both turn in Sheila's direction thinking she was awake and heard them speaking about Eddie Sr. But to their surprise Sheila is still sleeping. Shanae and Grandma Jean look at one another at the moment Sheila starts choking in her sleep. Grandma Jean rushes to her bedside trying to wake Sheila with light smacks to the face. "Shanae get some help," Grandma Jean requested.

Shanae darts out of the room to get help. Grandma Jean attempts to wake Sheila by smacking her yelling her name, "SHEILA!"

Sheila gasps for breathe and screams, "BYRANT NO!" Momma Jean slaps Sheila even harder. Sheila wakes up reaching for her mother's neck with both hands as if someone was choking her. She takes deep breathes trying to control her breathing. She looks at her mother with the strangest look.

"Are you okay? You had me quite scared. You alright?" Momma Jean asked.

Sheila appears in a daze, "I'm okay."

Dr. M. Duke runs to Sheila's bedside checking her vitals.

"How are you feeling Mrs. Fox?" Dr. M. Duke asked.

"It all just felt so real," Sheila replied.

"What felt so real?" Dr. M. Duke asked.

"My dreams. In my dream somebody was choking me and the next thing I knew that I was short of breathe," Sheila stated.

"With all that you have been through over the past few days you may experience more episodes similar to that. You are going to need some counseling to help deal with your stress level. It will help you deal with your anxiety," Dr. M. Duke said.

Dr. M. Duke leans forward with her stethoscope to listen to Sheila's heart, "Sit up for me. Your heart rate is a little fast. I need for you to think pleasant thoughts. Follow my finger please?" Dr. Duke takes a seat on Sheila's bed grabbing her hand, "I know news about a love one can be very tough. It affects people differently...."

Sheila interrupts Dr. Duke with a confused look.

"What news would that be?" Sheila asked.

Shanae and Grandma Jean look at one another.

"We hadn't told her anything yet Dr. Duke." Grandma Jean said nervously.

Sheila gets extremely loud, "TOLD ME WHAT?"

Shanae quickly walks out of the room. Grandma Jean approaches the bed grabbing Sheila's hand. Dr. Duke nods in approval for Mrs. Harris to break the news about Eddie Sr.

"Sweetie, Eddie is in a vegetative state," Mom Jean said.

Sheila's face turns red as the tears stream down her cheeks. Mom Jean sits on the bed to console her as Dr. Duke watches over Sheila.

Through Sheila's pain and tears she mumbles out, "Mom, it's all my fault. It's my fault. Mom it's my fault."

Mom Jean pulls Sheila's head down into her breast to quiet her.

"Dr. Duke Sheila will be just fine. Give us a minute please!"

Dr. Duke curious to what Sheila meant, "How is it your fault Sheila?"

Sheila just continues to cry in her mom's chest.

"Okay, Mrs. Harris. I'll leave you two alone." Dr. Duke rubs the top of Sheila's hand turns and walks out of the room.

"Mommy NO!" Sheila cried out.

"SShhhh!! It's not your fault," Mom Jean said as she watches Dr. Duke close the door behind her. Instantly Mom Jean snaps on Sheila lifting her head off her chest. "WHAT THE HELL DO YOU MEAN IT'S YOUR FAULT?"

Through Sheila's tears she tries to explain as her mother listens intently. "Well, Bryant and I came up with a plan…."

Momma Jean upset, "Really Sheila? What plan?"

Sheila went over every detail with her mother leaving nothing else to discover. Mom Jean just listens and rock back and forth in disbelief. Sheila cried like a newborn baby as she went on about the events and how they took place.

"What have I done? I'm so sorry. Mom, I screwed up. That's what I meant when I asked could the boys live without me."

Mrs. Jean sat there in the deepest of thoughts not saying a word while holding Sheila tightly.

Six months later Eddie Sr. is back home living with his parents in a wheelchair. Sheila had to move back home with her parents, because the medical bills were too high for her to manage the mortgage. The Feds had launched a full investigation on Eddie Fox after he got shot. They closed down Eddie's real estate office, confiscated the documents and seized all property leaving Sheila financially ruined.

The police still have no leads or clues about motives or suspects in Eddie's shooting not even six months later. Although, there were rumors circulating that it was Old Man Baker who set it up. Most thought that even Big Randy had sat it up to steal his own money just to keep Eddie Sr. in debt. Big Mike had his suspicion about Joe, because Joe was a true gambler who stayed in and out of debt. Joe who never trusted anybody but Eddie suspects all of them could have done it. Most of the guys stop hanging out gambling for a while. Joe decides it was time to make some money for his boy Eddie Sr. Joe hosts dice games at his house. The guys are standing around the pool-table nobody stood where Eddie Sr. normally would stand. Eddie called that spot lucky. Joe grabs the cup off the table and shakes the dice rolls out of the cup against the rail of the pool-table. Old Man Baker speaks out breaking the silence.

"What the fuck is this, a crap game or a funeral? You players are real quiet up in this bitch. This kind of shit makes a player nervous."

Big Mike rubs his face then speaks, "I feel you on that OMB. But real talk somebody in this room knows what happened to Eddie Sr. since nobody wants to bring it up."

Joe quickly swoops up the dice placing them back in the cup looking at Big Mike. The room went silent again as everyone gazed at one another. Joe snaps out, "MAN IF I FIND OUT ONE OF YOU PLAYERS HAD SOMETHING TO DO WITH MY GUY. IT'S GOING TO POP OFF."

Old Man Baker taken offense to it, "Joe this is why you brought us here to disrespect us?" Old Man Baker opens his jacket revealing his snub-nose 38 pistol. Joe pulls his 9mm from his lower back placing it on the pool table, "NOW WHAT?"

Big Mike intervenes, "Hold'em up fellas. None of us really know what happened but Eddie Sr. no sense in us killing one another or going to war for that matter. If something happens here tonight, it's going to be a war all over the city. None of us need that trouble or heat."

Old Man Baker nods in agreement and starts grabbing his money.

"I thought we were all 98 and two up in here. I was wrong things not 100 around here and will never be from this point on. Stay out of my land."

Big Mike frowns, "Like that OMB?"

Old Man Bakers exits quickly.

Big Mike shakes his head, "DAMN!"

Joe angry, "We shooting or what?"

"You were dead wrong for that," Big Mike stated.

"Fuck OMB! He ain't on shit," Joe said angrily.

Everybody started leaving Joe's house quickly. Joe had pissed the only man in the room off that no one wanted problems with. The crap game is over and Joe is sitting in his living-room pondering his next move his cell phone rings.

"What's good fam?"

"It's going down."

Joe quickly dashes out of the house to his vehicle peeling tires.

Over at the James' house, Sheila is sitting in the family room watching television with her parents. Papa James is flipping through, the channels he stops on WERK news.

"HI! I'm Michelle Matthews reporting LIVE from the north side of the city. Two men were gunned down as they exited club Baller's. As you can see behind me the Police have the area taped off. The gentlemen killed tonight were allegedly gang members. On this night a rival gang was having a birthday party for one of its members. As the two men attempted to get in there late model BMW, a car pulled alongside of them and open fired what was said to be an automatic weapon that unleashed fifteen to twenty shots. The two victims were Bryant and his cousin Shawn Fields, who both died at the scene. This is just another senseless murder in our streets. Michelle Matthews reporting live WERK Television back to you, Amber."

The Lottery drawing is up next on the news. Papa James looks around the room at Jean then Sheila. "Where's Reggie? That's his Buddy Bryant."

Momma Jean with little emotion looks at Sheila. "Reggie's out front with E.J."

Papa James jumps up out his seat to open the door and tell Reggie about the news. What he discovers when the door opens was Joe, Reggie and E.J. sitting on the porch.

Papa James frantic, "Get in here son. Your friend Bryant and his Cousin just got killed. It's on the news now."

The three of them head inside as the news recaps this time showing their pictures. "These two guys were at the wrong place at the wrong time. Both murdered outside club Baller's. That's your news for the night. I'm Michelle Matthews signing off."

Reggie looks at Sheila and gives her a slight nod. Sheila has a smirk on her face. Momma Jean just sits there with a blank look on her face, as Papa James surveys the whole room. Joe winks at Sheila and Papa James sees it happen. Sheila nods as if she approves of Joe's actions.

Reggie and Joe go back outside. Papa James sits around looking crazy at his wife and Sheila.

"What the hell is going on around here? Did I miss something?" Papa James asked.

Momma Jean replies, "Please! You never miss anything."

E.J. starts laughing. Sheila reaches out to E.J. pulling him up on the couch next to her.

"I'm serious. What's going on? Nobody seems surprised about Bryant. That Reggie didn't say a word, something funny round here," Papa James said.

They continue to watch television as if Papa James hadn't said a word.

Out in front of the house Joe and Reggie are sitting inside of Joe's truck. Joe opens the glove box with his key revealing ten thousand dollars. He grabs it passing it to Reggie.

"Naw Brah! I told you this one was on me," Reggie said.

Joe nods in agreement, "Yup! But this is yours."

"Besides, you went with me," Reggie said.

"I'm always down with a good cause. Take it," Joe replied.

They exchange daps and Reggie jumps out the car. Joe quickly pulls away as Reggie makes his way back into the house.

Later that evening on the other side of town Tonya stops by the Fox's home with her son Marcus. The Foxes have a beautiful suburban home.

Mrs. Fox walks in the room where Tonya is sitting next to Eddie while playing with her baby. Eddie is strapped into his wheelchair. Eddie has not made one ounce of progress since the shooting.

"Tonya, baby, I need to go by the store to pick up Eddie's prescriptions. Can you watch him while I run to the store?" Mrs. Fox asked.

"Oh that's no problem," Tonya replied.

"I really appreciate it. Herman should be home any moment he got caught in traffic. Anyhow, I'll be right back."

"Okay!" Tonya agreed.

Tonya is bouncing Marcus up in her lap, sitting right in front of Eddie Sr. "Weeee!!!" She pulls Marcus down turns him toward Eddie.

"Eddie this is our son Marcus," Tonya said.

Tonya continues to play with Marcus directly in front of Eddie.

Marcus starts to cry after about fifteen minutes of playing. She lifts him up to smell his back side.

"You're okay. You must be hungry?" Tonya said to Marcus.

She bends over in front of Eddie Sr. to go inside of her diaper bag. She grabs the baby bottle, pops the top off and the top lands on the floor. "Dang it!" Tonya said as she bent over to grab it.

She thinks she bumps Eddie's hand when she bends over. She stands straight up and feels something touch her butt again. At that moment she realizes that Eddie reached out to touch her butt. She quickly turns around to look at Eddie Sr. with a big smile, but he hasn't made another move. She places Marcus on her hip.

"Marcus! Your dad loves these buns! Look at him acting like he hasn't done anything." She lowers Marcus right in front of Eddie, "Eddie, touch our baby boy." At that moment Eddie grabs the baby's foot. Tonya excited kisses Eddie on the forehead.

She takes a seat right in front of Eddie. "We're going to be just fine." Eddie continues to move his hand. Tonya just smiles. At that very moment Tonya realizes that Mr. Fox and Sheila are standing in the doorway. Mrs. Fox so excited to see Eddie's hand moving and missed the entire conversation. However, Sheila sat there leaning on the wall contemplating her next move. Tonya had her own agenda thinking to herself, "Once Eddie makes a full recovery, we'll find out who was behind this robbery."

Sheila immediately walks over steps in front of Tonya and baby Marcus blocking them out from Eddie's view. Sheila kneels down in front of Eddie Sr. grabbing both hands, "Hey Sweetie! I see you're making progress. I saw your hand move. If you can understand what I'm saying Eddie move your hand again, please?"

Eddie is unresponsive to Sheila's demand. She stands walks over to Mrs. Fox. "Mom, I think that maybe at the moment Eddie's nerves in his hand just twitched."

Mrs. Fox with great disappointment, "He just has so much to live for." Mrs. Fox starts to tear up. Sheila embraces her mother-in-law. Tonya feelings are hurt she starts to pack up. She knows that Eddie's hand touched her butt. She bends over in Eddie's face again to grab the diaper bag and Eddie touches her butt.

"I know you could move your hand," Tonya said with excitement as Sheila and Mrs. Fox watched. Eddie's eyes move staring at Tonya's butt.

Sheila furious and Mrs. Fox confused. Sheila runs back over to Eddie Sr. He is trying to speak while Sheila kneels down in front of him blocking Tonya and Marcus. He mumbles out with a very weak voice.

"B..i…, mo…." Eddie said.

Mrs. Fox tears turn to tears of joy. She starts to pray silently as she looked on.

Sheila excited, "What are you saying Eddie?

Sheila grabs her water bottle to lubricate Eddie's throat. She holds the bottle pouring a little into his mouth. Eddie tries to speak again. Sheila is waiting ever so patiently on Eddie to gather his thoughts. Mrs. Fox looks on in amazement. Eddie's lips are dry he licks his lips and tries to speak again.

"B.it…mo.."

Sheila anxious, "I can't understand."

Tonya places her baby bag on her shoulder scoops up Marcus getting ready to leave.

Eddie yells out, "BITCH MOVE!"

Sheila's heart sank. She thought to herself, *Eddie knows what happen and what might he do or say?*

Mrs. Fox stunted stands with her mouth hung open. Tonya smirks and continues to exit, "I guess we'll find out what happened?" Guess who's SCORN now?

THE END

Be on the lookout for "SCORN 2"
The Legacy continues!

Kevin Whitaker's debut novel "The Party Girl".
Available at www.mcclurepublishing.com and other
leading book stores.

Special Thanks to **Joy Pearson** for being the first
to order both books "The Party Girl" and "SCORN".

www.ingramcontent.com/pod-product-compliance
Lightning Source LLC
Chambersburg PA
CBHW070955120726
47910CB00004B/1247